THE SPECIALIST

THE SPECIALIST

THE COSTA RICA JOB

CHARLES PETERSON SHEPPARD
As conceptualized by Phillip W. Sheppard

ARCHWAY
PUBLISHING

Archway Publishing books may be ordered through booksellers or by contacting:

Archway Publishing
1663 Liberty Drive
Bloomington, IN 47403
www.archwaypublishing.com
1-(888)-242-5904

This book is a work of fiction. Names, characters, locations, events, places, organizations and businesses are either the product of the author's imagination or used fictiously. Any resemblance to actual persons living or dead, events or locales is entirely coincidental.

Because of the dynamic nature of the Internet, any web addresses or links contained in this book may have changed since publication and may no longer be valid. The views expressed in this work are solely those of the author and do not necessarily reflect the views of the publisher, and the publisher hereby disclaims any responsibility for them.

Any people depicted in stock imagery provided by Thinkstock are models, and such images are being used for illustrative purposes only.

Certain stock imagery © Thinkstock.

Library of Congress Control Number: 2013902102

ISBN: 978-1-4808-0017-5 (sc)
ISBN: 978-1-4808-0019-9 (hc)
ISBN: 978-1-4808-0018-2 (e)

Printed in the United States of America

Archway Publishing rev. date: 2/1/2013

DEDICATION

Phillip Sheppard
The Specialist

I dedicate this to my son, Marcus,
whom I love very much, more than words can say.

I conceptualized and commissioned
this novel in memory of my
Great-Great-Great Grandfather, Jesome Herring,
and my mother, Ernestine Winona Sheppard,
and all my family, who have helped shape me into the person I am.

I wish to extend a special and loving thanks
to my brother, Charles Peterson Sheppard
for writing a story of fiction with a character and persona
who reminds me in so many ways of myself.
Thank you my brother. This book is only the beginning, man.

Phillip W. Sheppard

"The greatest strength can be a weakness, if properly exploited."

The Specialist

FOREWORD

Having the opportunity to meet Phillip Sheppard, *The Specialist*, at a past charity event was truly an honor. He is a man full of adventure, intelligence and charisma, with a charm and personality that feels contagious. Watching him on a nationally televised reality show provided me with my first impressions, but watching the very last episode allowed me to draw more distinct conclusions about who the man really is. Phillip's energetic personality radiates toward others. His sharp mind works constantly to analyze the situation, scan the environment, decipher those around him, and furnish a plan to make the best of all possible situations. That's why I like this book so much. It captures his essence. Being asked to read *The Specialist: The Costa Rica Job* was an honor equal to meeting the man himself.

As a published author (*Your Winner Within*), I know the effort involved in writing a book, and this novel truly surpassed my expectations. Once I picked the book up and began reading, I couldn't put it down. Loaded with excitement, anticipation, challenging situations and unanswered questions, this gem made me yearn to read faster, just to enjoy the final outcome. From the beginning, I tried predicting the finish, but the unexpected conclusion produced more than surprise; it served up a jaw dropping shock! The characters seem so real; I could actually visualize them and all the situations they encountered. This is a 'must read'.

This book will answer all your questions about who *The Specialist* really is. As I read it, I couldn't help but think about how proud I felt of Phillip. In conceptualizing this fictional work, he has fulfilled some lofty personal expectations.

It must be great to be *The Specialist*.

Holly Hoffman,
Author, Survivor Contestant: Nicaragua, Season 21, Motivational Speaker

CHAPTER 1

In hindsight, Mimi Sabo's phone call sparked my long-awaited return to form.

I never did let myself go completely—not even after the thirty-nine days of hell I endured in Costa Rica. That job paid more than it cost me, but still not enough to justify the injuries I received when a dirty cop named *Aguilera* and his drug-slinging friends boot-stomped me senseless one night. They snagged my wallet and passport of course, and then dumped me a hundred miles south in *Puerto Armuelles,* a city on the west coast of Panama. That's right, Panama. That's where they left me, slumped over on a dusty side street. I lost a few days too, but eventually I got myself right.

They didn't kill me so I guess I got off easy, but the bum's rush treatment took its toll.

I had no real recourse. It's not like I could run to an embassy or gripe to the tourist board, not in my line of work. Besides, sometimes you have to keep things in perspective. Rico Bravo, the 22-year-old kid I hired as a guide got it a lot worse than me. They arrested him on his way home somewhere in the province of *Limon,* Costa Rica and shortly thereafter, he got shot during a supposed 'escape attempt.' According to all the local media outlets, the shooter was the same dirty cop who sent me packing... *Aguilera.* I never talk much about what I do in the first place, and ever since young Rico Bravo died, I've clammed up a lot more. Costa Rica was the first job I ever did that went totally bad, my first major screw up. Getting back to the States in one piece did little to ease the sense of failure that followed me around like a black cloud. I felt guilty as hell about that Costa Rican kid, still do, and for a while I lost my edge.

So, I took six months off, completely.

I quit working out and picked up a few pounds and just shrugged it off. Eventually I got a grip, but by that time, my body needed a tune-up and an oil change, if not a complete overhaul. Lack of constant practice also downgraded my intuitive perception.

But I digress…

Mimi Sabo started calling the day before I received a Pay Rent or Quit notice for my small office space in Santa Monica. Not a big deal, I had been in that sling before.

When I walked into the office that day, my secretary Charity Fields had that worried look on her face, the one on display whenever we get a quit notice that coincides with her upcoming payday. Charity's a cute California blond, a mom who's chipper and mighty crisp at the desk work, with a five year old son to fend for. She had every right to worry about her finances and my obligations to them. We share a bond of mutual trust and support. She hadn't quit on me in seven years and I doubt she ever would, but she still had that worried look.

"Rent's due, boss…"

"Don't remind me. And don't worry, we'll make payroll. It's only you."

"Have to worry sometimes. It's not just me, you know that."

"I know…"

"Are we gonna be okay this time or should I just call my pimp and ask for extra weekend work?" We laughed and for a moment the worry went away.

"We're not quite there yet," I said. She wasn't exactly convinced. "And here I thought I was your only pimp, Charity…"

"A gal's gotta do what she's gotta do…If you can't look out for me boss, well…"

"Gee, thanks for the vote of confidence."

"It's just that things are slow. Loyalty won't put bread on the counter…"

"Yeah, that's true. Things are hard all over, I guess."

"You've been so mighty picky and choosy lately. You've been avoiding work."

"Have I?"

"Haven't you?"

I had. She knew it. I knew it. Funds were low. The onus was on me. I had to get back into the mix.

I sighed. "Any good calls, any inquiries…anything?"

"Well, there's been a woman calling since yesterday…not collections, either."

"How reassuring. Does she need a Specialist?"

"Absolutely."

"Then why didn't you say anything about it before now?"

"Because she said she's from Costa Rica."

"Oh…"

CHAPTER 2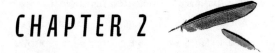

In my line of work I am known as a specialist.

For the past fifteen years, I have perfected my singular expertise in personal security, counter-terrorism, kidnap prevention, threat response, and of course physical combat. I have protected the rich, the famous, and the politically elite from the worst heavies you can possibly imagine... and at times I have been paid handsomely to do so.

Due to my unique skill set and my reputation for absolute discretion, most knowledgeable people refer to me simply as *The Specialist*. I am not alone. There are others like me, but I am exceptional... more highly recommended and more preferred than most. In fact, I am the most sought-after commodity in my profession. What is it I do? People often ask me that. My answer is seldom the same. Depending on whom you are, where you happen to be, the nature of your predicament and your financial resources, I am many things.

I am not a spy. I am not an assassin. I am no longer a government agent; I am none of the things that immediately come to mind to unimaginative people. Some say I am an eraser of sorts, but I don't eliminate people...I just make problems go away.

"As I am sure you can imagine, I would not go to such great lengths to find you if I had not already determined the expenses involved and your level of expertise. Mrs. Fields has grown quite annoyed with my persistence, I imagine."

Mimi Sabo's accent was thick, but her English was more than

passable. She looked young, right out of college, but more refined than American girls of the same age. She was beautiful and worldly, a rich foreign woman, and already sophisticated. I detected her dialect as not fully Costa Rican, at least not anymore. She had been educated, but probably not in her home country. Most of the Costa Rican public universities were technically oriented and most of the private schools focused on the biological sciences and medicine; she didn't come across as either type. Beyond her family history, I really did not know what to make of her. The clothes were the top of the line and she acted, for want of a better term, rich. She adorned her throat with a lovely multicolored gemstone necklace that looked handmade but very expensive.

"The neckpiece," I said, motioning toward it with a finger. "Did you pick it up in Brazil?"

"Yes. How did you know?"

"The gemstones...tourmaline. Unmistakable. Those particular color variations can only be found in Brazil, in the state of *Paraiba*. Students wear them as good luck charms, although not as nicely crafted as your own. Did you study there?"

She seemed momentarily surprised before smiling and nodding. "Yes, at the Federal University of Paraiba, but only briefly. If you have not already completed a background check of me, then you are very... perceptive... and well informed."

"I make my living being both, and yes I always determine who it is I might be working for before I decide to work for them. However, there was precious little information about your formal education to be found, unless Mrs. Fields is slipping, and I doubt that very seriously. Let's talk about what you think you need from me. I'd prefer you be—"

"To the point?"

"Exactly. I'm not easily shocked and if you've contacted me you should be well past the point of embarrassment or shame, if you have cause for any at all."

"Actually, I'm afraid..."

"Well at least you are doing something about that. That's a step. Talk to me. My time is limited…"

I really didn't buy Mimi Sabo's narrative, not completely, not in my Specialist gut. There was just something fishy about it. Her story seemed tragic enough but slightly rehearsed, too. It only needed a gung-ho hero to save the day. I felt ill-suited for that role, especially if she was holding something back. I was prepared to decline the job until she placed a twenty-five-thousand dollar cashier's check on the edge of my desk.

That certainly re-ignited my interest.

It also made for good drama, so I decided to up the ante.

"Young lady I hope you know, for me that's barely an advance…"

She looked stunned.

I wish I could have seen the unflinching look on my own face. It had to be classic to shake her up the way it did.

"All that money is just an advance? Just a down payment?"

"Well, given the logistics involved, the inherent dangers to life and limb, the overall risk, developing contacts, securing safe lines of communication, the cost of payoffs and bribes, not to mention my personal expenses…yeah, what's on the table right now won't cut it."

"I, well, I…that is, um… I assumed that would be enough."

"It's not. That check will only get me standing on a helicopter landing pad next to a jungle path in *Xiomara*, Costa Rica —by myself— hopefully without being detained by some minister of public security, or worse, the United States military. One man trekking through that jungle with a .32 Tomcat pistol tucked between his butt-cheeks will not get it done." I pointed out to her that the commercial flights were simply out of the question for the type of activity she wanted performed. "Homeland Security, the U.S. Air Force, Customs, the drug cartels, they all keep tabs on who's flying in and out of these small Central American countries. The four international airports and the smaller domestic ones are completely out of the question. Even the little private landing strips report unusual activity, unless there's quiet money paid up front. There's no getting around it. I learned that the hard way, believe me. It's a lesson I don't need repeated."

"I have learned things the hard way too. I don't need lessons repeated either…" We bantered and haggled about her generosity and my apparent lack of gratitude, and though I sorely needed the money, my stubborn indifference apparently threw her off a bit. Eventually, she grew impatient, copped a nasty attitude and placed her hand on the cashier's check like she was pulling the offer from the table. The glimmer of irritation in her eyes and the slight flush to her bronze skin made her seem more alluring, if that was even possible, while the bright tourmaline gemstones around her neck glittered more intensely with each agitated movement. "I was hoping so badly this would be the solution," she said. 'But I was wrong, because like so many other people, you just want the money. You will help the rich and the powerful, and that's all."

"Look, Miss Sabo this is not a shake down, it's reality. Wake up. I didn't fly twenty-five hundred miles to ask you for work. You flew here. I'm a businessman. I work for the wealthy because that is where the money is, not because I like them, necessarily. Criminals target the rich for the same reason. If you don't want my services and you can find someone else who'll listen to your story and work cheap, by all means do so. I'm sure there's someone out there who'll gladly take your money and walk around Costa Rica on your dime. Good luck with that. You probably won't even miss that twenty-five thousand, right? But will cutting corners grant you peace of mind or solve your problem? No, not without real results it won't. That's what matters…results. That's basically what I provide, but I don't work cheap, that's all."

She seemed a little taken aback. I could tell she had grown accustomed to flashing money at people and watching them jump through hoops.

She bit her lower lip and took a moment to consider my viewpoint.

"Fine then," she said at last, leaning back in her chair, pretending to relax. "You say that this check is an advance. How much exactly will your services cost me?" She stared at me calmly and coolly and then smoothly crossed her legs. I suddenly realized she was wearing a short business skirt…and that she was exquisitely equipped to do so.

I lifted my gaze and stared back at her. Closers always know when to close.

"I think a hundred and twenty-five thousand dollars will be sufficient. That's what I usually charge for an operation of this sort. No guarantees, but you have my word that I'll do everything I can to get the job done."

"Then the twenty-five thousand dollar cashier's check is good for the advance, like you said, with the remainder to be paid later? I want things to be very clear."

"No… I'll need one-hundred-thousand dollars up front. I hope that's clear. It's an absolute necessity, not greed. Times are hard all over. I have a lot of preparation to do in a short amount of time. Twenty-five thousand dollars, later… that will be fine."

"Assurance?" she asked. "Peace of mind?"

I nodded. "Something like that."

She leaned forward and pulled the twenty-five thousand-dollar cashier's check from my desk and secured it inside her purse. Then without further delay, she pulled out another cashier's check and laid it down.

I glanced at the amount. It was for one-hundred-thousand-dollars. It was my turn to be stunned. She clearly cherished my expression, and then finally came clean.

"Your reputation precedes you, sir…"

"Wow," I said dryly. "I guess I am not the only one doing my homework…"

CHAPTER 3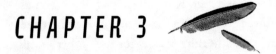

I knew if I returned to Costa Rica, I would do myself a big favor to establish better intelligence links, with facts and knowledge about the local politics. No matter how good the operative, he must have good intelligence. Sharp eyes and keen ears only get you so far.

I decided to contact another Specialist, Ze'ev Pinsky, formerly of the Israeli Defense Forces (IDF), a past employee of Israel Aerospace Industries (IAI) and an ex-member of Israel's secret service, Mossad.

Ze'ev's U.S. friends called him Zeff, but he preferred the Israeli pronunciation, which translated to 'wolf.' As a master of the martial art Krav Maga, his name suggested a naked aggression that Ze'ev could definitely summon in the proper circumstances. Simply put, Ze'ev Pinsky was one hard-fisted, bad-ass Jew—and he liked it when I told him so. He was smart too. In the late 80's he helped install electronic sensors on the Lavi jet fighter aircraft (until the United States nixed funding to eliminate Israel's rival to the F16). He spent another portion of his career bugging embassies and hotels across the Middle East, including some occupied by Israel's closest allies.

But he was also something more.

In my profession, he was the closest thing I had to a friend.

We had met twenty-five years earlier at a mixed martial arts seminar sponsored by different branches of the intelligence community, long before anybody thought to package the concept as a TV gladiator sport. The goal at the time was to develop a comprehensive discipline that functioned as both an offensive and defensive fighting system for field operatives. Ze'ev headed up a unit from Israel and I came along as the top student of a U.S. Wing Chun Kung Fu school. Back in those days I was a 'ripped to shreds bad-ass' in my own right, with attitude to spare. We came away with a healthy respect for each other's skills. However, if forced to tell the truth, I think Ze'ev would have admitted that Wing Chun proved the superior fighting system. Still, over the years we remained colleagues, not rivals, sharing intelligence and collaborating on occasion to our mutual benefit.

Ze'ev had informed me on a prior occasion, months before in fact, that he had once tailed a Hezbollah operative moving between Honduras and Brazil who mysteriously broke pattern and entered a small bank in *San Jose*, Costa Rica. He never determined the Hezbollah operative's motives, but my story sparked his keen interest. Naturally, he requested a complete briefing. I was happy to oblige.

He came by later, the same afternoon I met Mimi Sabo.

He always liked Charity Fields, so upon arrival he stopped by her desk and flirted a bit. I think she may have liked him too because she made a point to tidy up her work area and brush her hair before he arrived. She never did that for anyone else. I always notice little things like that. They certainly did not lack for conversation.

"Mr. Pinsky, this new case is right up your alley," said Charity, at last.

"So are you Mrs. Fields," said Ze'ev charmingly. "So are you."

"I saw that line coming a mile away," I said loudly from my office. "By the way, Ze'ev…I have to call my son, make sure he's on point, is that cool?"

'Sure…take your time. And how is little Malcolm?"

"Fine, thanks, just not so little anymore."

I figured I'd let Charity and Ze'ev catch up before we briefed. I called Malcolm. I let his cell phone ring once, and then hung up. Malcolm called back seconds later. The ritual had no real purpose; it was just our little thing ever since he completed a sixteen week stint at a National Guard youth academy called Sun Crest. I had signed him up for Sun Crest after he got into a series of fights at school. Kids wanted to fight him just because he studied martial arts like his old man. He never started the fights, but he knew how to end them, usually in dramatic fashion.

"Sorry dad," said Malcolm, after the last kid got rushed to the Santa Monica Hospital over on 15th Street. "He came at me, so I had to go. When I go I go hard, just like you told me to."

I indeed had said that, and it's a philosophy I'll never abandon, but was it fair? I'm a Specialist, he was not. He was a kid in school. Right or wrong, I decided to remove him from the situation. That's why he ended up at Sun Crest. He hated me at first, and said I made him look like a loser, because that's all who went to Sun Crest, but I knew I had to do it. In the end he completed the academy with honors.

I was so proud of him. But I still kept tabs on him, kept inside his head. I still had to be his father, because he would always be my son. Somehow we always muddled through together.

"What's up, boy," I asked.

"Nothing'…just chillin'"

"I bet I know what you were doing…" He sounded preoccupied at that moment.

"No you don't…"

"Yeah I do…" The television was on. I heard it even as he turned down the volume a little more.

"Okay. What am I doing…?"

"Call of Duty, Black Ops…I know you, man."

"No, sorry, I'm watching this DVD you gave me."

"Which one?"

"That one about, um…Wing Chun butterfly knives and the long dragon pole…"

"Oh, that one. Cool. You like?"

"I like the butterfly knives, but I'm not gonna be carrying' 'round no pole, Dad."

"True, but it's a good balancing trainer. House clean?"

"Yeah…"

"No, it's not…"

"Well, I started….It'll get done."

"Yeah okay, blah-blah-blah…Ze'ev Pinsky… 'member him? He's here, says hi."

"Cool. Tell him I think I can take him now."

"Yeah, right. Hey, what's the best fighting style?"

I knew he loved to watch Krav Maga on YouTube so I had to ask, because after twenty-five years Ze'ev refused to give Wing Chun it's due.

"The best fighting style? Total invisibility. Can't be beat, Dad…"

"Okay, okay. I can't argue that. Not too many people have mastered that style, though. So what's the second best fighting style?"

He thought a long time before answering.

"Wing Chun Kung Fu… your style, Dad…right?"

CHAPTER 4

We both adopted semi-professional tones during briefings…just habit.

"I'll be operating in your old back yard, Ze'ev," I said. "You taught Krav Maga in *Limon* and in San José, right?"

"Absolutely," said Ze'ev, nodding firmly. "I know both cities and their surrounding terrain very well. Both are just big towns, really."

"Agreed," I said. "Both have some pretty raw spots."

"Yeah, very rough, lots of poverty, prostitution, youth crime. A lot more dangerous than your average tourist cares to imagine. I still have a small training center in *San Jose*."

"Still? I wish I had known that the last time."

"Yeah, I bet. I also still have a full blown fighting school in *Limon*. About twenty of the students are living right there on the grounds. They are at your complete disposal. One of them is active Mossad, two others are IDF reservists and very dependable. One is CIA, but he will not lift a finger to help you. CIA are very restricted in what they can do abroad…useless, really. You can tell the CIA man and anyone else who asks that you are a visiting Kung Fu master and, if necessary, kick their ass to prove it. No one there can take you one on one. There is a small armory beneath the school if you need anything." He chuckled. "Wonderful things…"

"Excellent."

Having Ze'ev aboard equated to gaining access to practically any weapon and communication device imaginable, even some in the experimental stages. That is what made his involvement and input so crucial to me.

"I will tell my IDF friends to look for you," said Ze'ev.

"That's comforting," I stated. "I recorded my interview with Mimi Sabo. You're welcome to hear it."

He frowned and shook his head. "Hmm...forgo that. What's Little Rich Girl's story...Daddy didn't come home from the whore house?"

"Not exactly. A lot more interesting than that. It's why I contacted you."

"Okay. Proceed..."

"Her father is vice president of *El Banco Puro*, in Costa Rica. His name is Juan Miguel Sabo. According to Miss Sabo, for the past three years her father has been an informant for the Ministry of Public Security and also for Interpol.

"Six weeks ago authorities arrested Antonio Pascal, the bank president. They also raided and searched multiple properties he owns in Costa Rica, Honduras and the United States, looking for financial records. Pascal is now in custody on a six month hold, accused of laundering millions of dollars through his bank for...*el Norte del Valle Cartel*...or the North Valley Cartel...Columbia."

"The new coke gods..." said Ze'ev.

"It would seem. He is also accused of doing the same for FARC."

"FARC...the communist rebels in Columbia and northern Brazil...." said Ze'ev. I could see the wheels turning in his head. "Two questions..."

"I'll try to answer them, if I can..."

"Why did Sabo turn on his boss instead of just asking for a cut?"

"According to Mimi Sabo, Pascal had an affair with her mother. I guess mama Sabo left papa Sabo and now resides in a Honduran hacienda owned by Pascal"

"That's why he went to Interpol?" asked Ze'ev. "For revenge?"

"Apparently so," I said.

"Why didn't he just walk into Pascal's office and slash his throat and then zip down his pants and cut off his balls? That's how these things are handled in the Middle East. What a coward...my other question is, did she have any idea exactly how the money was laundered?"

"Well, Mrs. Fields did some research this afternoon." I said. "Apparently the bank president bought up dozens of soccer stadiums throughout Central and South America, all bush league stadiums. He made it look like all these stadiums were selling out to capacity, so a stadium with an average attendance of, say two thousand, looked like it sold ten thousand tickets per game. Clever, and very legit-seeming. It worked for years. By the way, the bank has been shut down and all assets frozen. Some people are extremely upset about that, I bet."

"Yeah," said Ze'ev, "Antonio Pascal, the North Valley Cartel, FARC...they all want that guy's head now."

"Yeah, and the plot thickens... Mimi Sabo's father was kidnapped one week ago. She said a local police officer contacted her family—very up front these people—and told her to come up with two million U.S. dollars within ten days. You know how the rest goes, don't you?"

"Does the girl have any idea where her father might be?

"She thinks somewhere in or around the capital, *San Jose.* I have about eight days to find him and try to extract him. You'd think the Costa Rican government would help."

Ze'ev nodded. "You know what's interesting? Remember that Hezbollah operative I trailed into a bank? The name of that bank was *El Banco Puro.*"

"Mmm..."

"If you don't mind, I'd like to contact my people down there, have them do recon. Just one day, while you get ready to move. It might be worth both our time."

"Agreed, thinking the same thing, Ze'ev."

"Great minds always think alike..."

CHAPTER 5

After the briefing, the three of us left the office together. My bank closed in an hour so I gave Charity the check. I didn't have to tell her what to do, she already knew.

"You know I'm on it, Boss. I'll be drumming my fingers at the teller's window before you hit the first traffic light. Guess we'll keep the doors open after all."

"Amen to that," I said.

Ze'ev chuckled softly. "Feeling better now, are you Mrs. Fields?"

"Um…yes," said Charity, stopping at her car. "Boss is on point again. Just look at him…he's hungry, and I'm glad about it. That's when he's at his best." She entered her vehicle, turned the engine over and rolled down her window. "See you guys later…and Ze'ev stop staring at me so hard or you'll burn a hole in something." She laughed in a way I had not heard in a while, then waved goodbye and drove away.

A black Tesla Roadster sat parked near my blue Beemer Z4. "Is that how you're getting around now Ze'ev? Very cool…is it brand new?"

"No, I bought it used. It's all electric…it's green."

"Yeah, I'm sure you bought it for its small environmental footprint, not because it looks hot and goes fast."

Nothing could have been further from the truth. I had no doubt Ze'ev had installed a host of electronic countermeasures as well.

"Speaking of footprints," I added, "I didn't know *Mossad* had an informal presence in Central America. Isn't Costa Rica outside of Tel Aviv's sphere of influence?"

"Do you think *Mossad* would be there without the knowledge and consent of the United States?"

I shook my head. "No. I'm not that naïve…"

"Of course you're not. But you might be surprised to learn how long they've been there, and I'm not talking about hunting down ninety-year-old Nazi scum. The world is getting smaller, my friend."

"Yeah…and look" I said, observing two unpleasant looking men coming our way, "it's getting meaner by the minute."

Hostiles incoming…

They both wore loose summer suits, the kind that look heavy but are not. One man pointed and grunted an indistinct command and as they drew closer their shoes slapped softly on the asphalt. They stopped a few short paces away and tried to stare us down… fat chance. It was their move then. They seemed undecided.

"The girl," said the older one, finally, in a menacing tone. I could tell he grew up speaking Farsi, but had traveled here and there. "Mimi Sabo. We follow her. She meet with you here, we know. Where is she now?"

"I couldn't tell you," I said.

"You lie." His eyes narrowed and his lower lip jutted out as he set his jaw and frowned. "You mean you won't."

Ze'ev spoke before I could respond. "He's not inclined to. Neither am I. Who the hell are you?"

The man shifted his eyes to Ze'ev. "Not important." He then returned his gaze to me. "You… your life *is* important though, yes? So I ask you one time more. Mimi Sabo?"

"I don't like being threatened," I said coolly.

Suddenly, with an awkward twist of their wrists, a shiny blade sprang from each man's jacket sleeve. It seemed quite surreal. The only place I had ever seen spring-loaded wrist knives was in a Hollywood movie.

That's how I knew they were amateurs.

"Friends of yours?" asked Ze'ev.

"Nope. If they were," I said, "not anymore."

They closed the gap. One came at me, the other at Ze'ev. We both assumed the defensive stances of our disciplines. My hands were bladed, palms up, with my inner arms facing my body for added protection. If my attacker sought to come in straight I could block and parry, or step aside quickly and turn the tables with a flanking combo or a devastating strike to his head. If he started swinging like a wild man, I might get cut—but it would be his last knife fight.

My mind and body merged as I crouched on the balls of my feet, watching his waist, his shoulders, his elbows and hands, anything that would reveal his intentions.

His combat skills seemed limited, but I never underestimate anybody.

"The girl," growled the man. He began lunging and jabbing and shifting back and forth, weak moves that I easily avoided. "The girl, we only want the Sabo girl!"

Why Mimi Sabo, I wondered.

"You better stay back," I warned, dead serious.

He actually froze for a moment when I spoke—'this door is wide open now'—but my reaction time had slowed due to time off, plain and simple. He recovered and swung at the air as I aborted my move. *Damn, I blew that...*

I stayed focused and regrouped; I heard the struggle behind me but never shifted attention from my foe. I noticed the little things—the dark mole near his ear, the deep gouge lining his jaw, the wrinkles, the way his eyes darted and danced—every detail was noted and filed away, every little move recorded and analyzed. I felt no fear; he was no match for me, we both knew that. His moves grew lackluster and un-inspired as reality settled in. Finally he gasped and lunged, desperately thrusting the blade forward. I had already 'read his telegraphs' and instantaneously twisted my torso accordingly.

The shiny blade passed by, throat high. His now-useless weapon floated in the air before me. I snatched and clutched his wrist from above and below, then bent it backward so the blade pointed back at him. He moaned when his tendons gave but I drove on, throwing him completely off center. I could have easily forced the blade into the soft, pulsing crease of his throat, but stabbed his shoulder instead. He shrieked like a crow in a rat trap and swung at me with his free hand.

"Oh, you want more?" I poked his eye stiffly with two blunt fingers, double-punched his chin, and took him down with a nasty finishing leg sweep. His head hit the pavement with a solid thud. That took the fight right out of him.

I glanced quickly over at Ze'ev, and his man was out cold. The strange, metallic wrist mechanism and the shiny blade it carried lay harmlessly on the ground next to him.

"Aw, party's over," said Ze'ev. "Elegant work though, Phillip. Nice moves."

I nodded, not fully pleased. "A little choppy," I confessed.

"You're excused. Now to find out who these buffoons are," said Ze'ev. He rummaged through the pockets of his man. "Wrist knives... comic book amateurs! This one still has his passport...forged? No, guess not...but well, well..."

"Who is he?" I glanced back at the one I demolished. He was still groggy.

"According to this, he's Hamid Iraj Safi, 17. Malcolm's age. Just a kid, really."

"Never heard of him," I said, "where's he from?"

"He's from Costa Rica by way of Iran, believe it or not."

"They looked related...this one's way older." I nudged my man with a foot.

"Ohh," he moaned.

"Who are you," I demanded, "who sent you?"

"Please...I am hurt..."

"Nobody cares," I hissed. He sure had some nerve. "Answer my questions!"

"Maziar Safi...the other is just my son. Please, do not hurt me. I only wanted the girl...the Sabo girl."

"What for?"

"They stole my money, all of it...all of it!" He started to whimper, but not for his son lying unconscious on the ground. "My money... my money!"

"Creep," I muttered, in disgust.

"Take his passport, if he still has it," said Ze'ev. "I'll run them both."

CHAPTER 6

Ze'ev conducted multi-agency inquiries through Data Call's latest software and the FBI's eGuardian system—integrated into his Tesla's onboard display—and got a quick hit on Maziar Safi ...nothing huge, just multiple priors for bank and wire fraud. However, his son Hamid Safi popped up as an associate of Iran's Jundallah, or 'Soldiers of God.'

"Hmm...young foot soldier. What do you know about them?" asked Ze'ev.

"Jundallah? Not much," I said. "They're rebels. They're fighting the Iranian government. I know that. They used to get money from the U.S. because they opposed Tehran. Then the leader and his brother got captured and hanged, about what, a year ago? After that, the U.S. flip-flopped. It suddenly declared Jundallah a terrorist organization."

"Just like that?"

"Yeah, all of a sudden," I said. "Right after they lost their go-to-guy."

"Turn 'em and burn 'em," said Ze'ev, "a classic case."

"Looked like it to me," I said. "What do you want to do with these two?" I looked at the two Iranians... face down, hands behind their heads, ankles crossed. "The father's a straight crook. You can't believe anything he says. I doubt the kid will be much help. "

"We'll see," said Ze'ev. I'm calling somebody right now."

The responders were not local police or paramedics; I assumed they were some branch of Homeland Security, maybe FBI. Their cars looked federal, not state, and their response time was decent. Once the 'suits' arrived I quietly disengaged and let Ze'ev explain things. I stood off to the side, but one suit took notice and tried to stare me down with a 'nothing to see here…move along' look. I stared right back at him. The day I let a Fed intimidate me is the day I need to find a new job. When Ze'ev caught my eye I signaled my departure with a subtle hand movement. He signaled back for contact later.

A Specialist does not dwell on exploits, it's counterproductive. The here and now matters more. I put the 'wrist knife exhibition bout' behind me and moved on. Needless to say, I had questions churning in my own mind. Mimi Sabo had answers, I suspected, and I knew right where to find her…

But first, I drove home to my apartment complex, The Shores, just off Ocean Park Boulevard near the beach. It's a nice place if you can afford it. It's a nice place if you can't afford it, too. A few of the tenants prove that on the first of each month.

I showered and changed into a pair of black Prada slacks, black Aldo shoes and a white Armani shirt, then dug through my watch drawer and selected a vintage black-faced, diamond-studded ESQ precision timepiece. I put on a few other tasteful pieces as well, all acquired over the years, like the pure silver feather that I wore around my neck so often. I have never liked too much attention, but I have always admired quality.

Later, when my son Malcolm arrived home, I slipped him some cash and told him to hit the Promenade that night, on me. He stuffed the one hundred dollar bill in his pocket like a grocery store receipt, and I fought the urge to lecture him about taking care of his money. He interpreted my gesture as spontaneous generosity until I informed him of my imminent—and nonspecific—travel plans. He then realized I had taken an assignment. If it bothered him, I could not really tell. He seemed to take it in stride, which made me agonize over how accustomed he had grown to my numerous excursions.

He deserved better. Raising him had certainly made me a better Specialist.

For one thing, he was not my clone, thank God. I don't believe I could live in harmony with an identical version of myself, much as it pains me to admit that. Like me, Malcolm possessed an exceptionally strong will of his own. I had grown to accept and embrace that…eventually. I had to learn patience first, though. You can't use 'advanced interrogation' tactics or deviant forms of torture on your own kid, at least not in the section of Santa Monica where I live. It's frowned upon. I also had to learn how to listen more and bark orders less…make sacrifices, not just demands, and bite my tongue instead of lashing out with it. Ultimately, Malcolm inspired my humanity, even though I chose a profession in which being humane is the last thing on anybody's mind.

Fatherhood did not really soften me.

It did make me question violence as an end-all tool of persuasion. It also made me long for a certain spiritual calm, and I believe those intangibles made me altogether different— and much better. Granted, sometimes brute force is the only option. You can't avoid that situational reality. But the more you emphasize intellect over brawn, the more options appear at your fingertips.

That's what my kid helped me bring to the table. I have to look at myself daily and judge my performance as a man and a father, not just a Specialist. In regards to that, Malcolm's eyes are my mirror; they seldom distort the truth. Looking back over the years, I think I did okay.

"You want me to drop you off at the Promenade?"

"You don't have to do that, Dad."

"I really don't mind, champ…"

"No Dad, I can walk or call a friend…really."

"Sure about that? I'm taking the yellow Enzo…sure you don't want a ride?"

"In the Ferrari …Sure." That did the trick. I know my son. He played it down, but inside he was clicking his heels and doing a back flip. "Let's roll…"

"Yeah but like I said, only to the Promenade…well, maybe down a side street or two but that's it."

We took a sweet spin and I burned some rubber in a few choice spots. He seemed to like that. Then I gave him my 'please don't trash the car' speech before I put him behind the wheel and let him cruise the Enzo to the Promenade.

Yeah, I'm a risk taker by nature.

He made it without a hitch. He gave me a brief history of Italian motor sports too, so once again I learned something from the kid. I didn't tell him my ultimate travel destination, of course. He may have wondered, but he never asked. Like me, he had selective curiosity. And no…the yellow Ferrari Enzo was not mine. I wish. It belonged to an Intellectual Property attorney who had business in Australia and asked me to tend to his Pony. I figured he wouldn't have given me his keys if he didn't want me to drive his car.

CHAPTER 7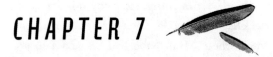

Sometimes the mind plays tricks.

You think you've seen somebody, but maybe you haven't, or have you? You head trip, begin pondering...start whispering in the attic. Somewhere along the line you convince yourself, or 'un-convince' yourself, that you didn't see what you thought you saw. Yeah, it happens.

I had just left Malcolm at the 3rd Street Promenade, turned right onto Ocean Avenue and stopped at Wilshire... red light, left lane. The Fairmont Hotel was just up ahead. I needed to swing right soon to get there, but a fender-bender had tied up my side of the intersection. The light turned green and the opposing traffic started passing through. I wasn't going anywhere soon.

A pearly white Cadillac Escalade rolled by...two men inside. I scanned their faces, no big deal, just a casual thing—and just about shit a brick... *Aguilera*!

Pardon my French ladies, but yeah, you heard right...*Aguilera*, sitting pretty and looking serene in the Escalade's passenger seat. Or was he? That's what I'm talking about... instant uncertainty.

Not *Aguilera*, the sadistic swine who ordered my beat-down—and smiled the whole time? No...not him...not the one who laughed out loud and howled, *"Costa Rica es mi Casa! No vengas otra vez, Puta."*

'Puta' is about the worst thing you can call a man. Nobody likes being called a pussy. It's even worse when the men who just pasted you to the pavement all laugh and agree unanimously.

You don't forget that, but I still told myself I was seeing things.

I convinced myself that he was just a mirage, a glitch in my mental software. I banished the whole 'victim thing' from my mind and re-turned to Specialist mode. I had work to do. Soon enough, I made my way to the Fairmont Hotel, where Mimi Sabo had booked a room. At the valet service, a young Asian man eyed the Ferrari, and looked me over as he took my keys. I ignored him. The man at the front desk reacted the same way. He gave up Mimi Sabo's bungalow location for less than a song, all because of the look...like always. Then, as an afterthought, he brazenly asked who I was.

"Singleton," I said, cocking my head a tad, as if he had no business posing the question. I pulled out a solid gold card holder and handed him a business card from a small Santa Monica record company called Spin/Move. "Jarred Singleton, vice-president... and who might you be?" He said nothing. I turned and headed to the secluded luxury bun-galows, with their graceful French doors and tranquil patios. I knocked on Mimi Sabo's door, and glanced back at the sky-blue pool and the lush landscaping. How lovely...

A women's voice called out, "Who's there?"

"The Specialist you hired today, Ms. Sabo. I'm alone. Open the door, please."

She looked like Mimi Sabo, just older and somehow more volup-tuous. She wore a form-fitting silk robe and sandals that exposed her arches and her long toes. Her hair swam and cascaded around her face in waves, very full and dark, and surely not dyed because a few gray strands mingled with all the rest. I liked her look; it fit the exquisite luxury of the suite's interior, partially visible behind her. Her dark lips were glossed, not painted, and though tell-tale smoker's lines had settled in, they still looked nice and full. The robe did its best to conceal her curves.

"If you are looking for Mimi, she is not here."

Her accent was strong, too. She looked me over and her eyes stared intently into mine. I could tell she was not the smiling type, but she liked what she saw as much as I did. "She said you were lean and tall and handsome. You are..."

"Thanks," I said. "Where is she? I need to talk to her."

"She went to work out, and maybe to the spa. She will return soon, I think. Do you need her telephone number?"

"No." I shrugged while taking her all in again. "I tried it. Straight to message every time. Are you two related?" The answer was obvious.

"Of course...everyone says we look alike."

"Older sister?"

"...Her mother. Thank you." I thought as much, but why not curry favor?

"Robó tiempo," I said. She smiled at my effort and allowed me to enter.

"So, I am a thief of time? And what are you, a thief of hearts?"

"On occasion... I really do need to speak to your daughter."

"I can try to call. She usually answers for me."

"Thanks." The place was fabulous to say the least, the kind for which you are expected to marvel and act deeply impressed. So I did, and it seemed to stroke her upper-class ego. Eventually, I noticed a seventeen inch MacBook Pro, gleaming on a mahogany desk-table. "Impressive. Does that notebook come with the room?"

"Oh no, that is Mimi's *computadora.* I was reading the Tico Times online..."

"Really? What's the weather like back home?" She was walking toward the laptop and I followed politely. "Lots of rain?"

"Yes. I was actually looking at the social calendar," she said. I should have known. "I thought I left my phone here..." She hadn't. "Where is it?"

I declined when she offered a seat on the sofa and watched her move about the bungalow looking for her phone. She swayed when she walked and moved with the calm confidence of a 'featured dancer' I once met. I wondered if she had great legs like her daughter Mimi... probably so, just thicker and meatier...not a deal breaker. She exited to the patio area and I glanced back at the MacPro screen. I wanted to see what things interested her.

I heard her say, "Ah," as if she had found her phone and just then I noticed a another web page on the MacBook, tabbed behind the main page, titled *Aguilera* Takes PCD Rank. Naturally, I grabbed the mouse and clicked.

My man *Aguilera* had just been promoted to Deputy Director of PCD, the narcotics division of Costa Rica's *Fuerzo Publica* —the state cops. I saw his picture too, erasing all doubt. Mimi Sabo or her mother—or both—knew him, unless it was all coincidence, everything, including my earlier sighting, but I no longer doubted myself. Even as my head swirled, I heard her talking in Spanish and managed to pick up most of it. I noted her tone and detected no stress. Her daughter had left the gym and moved on to the spa; I understood that much. I restored her web page. When she finished she returned and sat down on the far side of the sofa.

"She's at the spa..." She crossed her legs and the robe slid open to expose a cinnamon thigh. She modestly corrected the slippage and pulled a cigarette from a small box lying on the sofa's arm. The robe began inching off her thigh again. I pretended not to notice and so did she. "Do you mind if I smoke, sir?"

I did. "No, not at all, feel free," I said. "I'm not paying for the room."

"It's electric. There is no smoke, just vapor, and of course nicotine." She dragged on the plastic cigarette and a red LED simulated the burning end. "Flavored vapor," she explained. She exhaled thoroughly, perhaps for my benefit. "This flavor is called '*Cereza Oscura.*'

"Dark Cherry?" I asked.

"Si. ¿Quiere el olor de cereza?"

"Yes, I like the smell of cherry. Absolutely...freshly picked and not over-ripe, early in the season. Of course, in regards to your dark cherry—the flavored vapor, I am inclined to think it refers to coffee. I detected that in the aroma...yes?"

"Yes, coffee comes from dark cherries," she said. "Coffee beans are the seeds."

"Interesting fact. Now before your daughter gets back, tell me this. Why are you here? She told me you left your husband for Pascal some time ago…"

"It's true I left my husband …but I still care about him."

"Your husband was cooperating with the police against Pascal. What's the deal? Keep it real. I just cashed a one-hundred-thousand dollar check. I'm betting it's your cash, not Mimi's."

"Yes…"

"Well, if you want your money's worth, I need to know everything."

"My husband and Pascal, they were best friends once. Both became bad men." She took another drag from her e-cig and blew out the sweet coffee aroma. "I am drawn to bad men and I hate myself for it…"

"Yeah? Bad men with money and power…there are worse things to hate yourself for, don't you think?" She thought about it, and then laughed.

"Perhaps you are correct. Mr. …"

"I'm a Specialist… that's all you really need to know. You paid. I work for you, not anybody else, not even your daughter."

"Yes…very well. Please rescue my husband. He is still my husband, even if we both made mistakes. He was kidnapped because he stole people's money."

"Who's money? That's usually good to know."

"I have no names…just powerful people who trusted him. Now the money is gone. I do not know how much, either. But it was a lot, a lot more than I am paying you. If you do this, you will not be making the world a better place. But Mimi will get her father back, until they kill him at last…maybe all of us."

"Well I can tell you this firsthand, they're coming for you all. You need to call hotel security and have them talk to the front desk or maybe quietly change venues. I had no problem locating you, and your daughter is being followed, too. Now in other news... *Santino Aguilera*... that name ring a bell?"

"No."

"*Aguilera*. Think again."

"I don't know him exactly...my daughter was contacted by a policeman named *Aguilera*, that's all I can say. She said he is only trying to help us, and that he is an important man. He is not the one who demanded money...he is clean, she said."

I believed her, but decided right then I didn't need to talk to Mimi Sabo. I probably wouldn't get an honest string of words from her mouth anyway. I took another hard look at her mother. She was indeed beautiful, and probably quite the blowtorch in bed, but a real piece of work, too.

"Look," I said, "I already got my money, most of it anyway. I can deliver the goods on a job like this, trust me. Just one thing, and listen good. From here on out, I contact you, nobody else."

"Understood...and what about this ...*Aguilera*?"

"Play dumb. We never spoke about him. If he helps you, great, but I somehow doubt he will. I'm going to program your cell phone to identify me with a special ring tone...let me see it...there...hear that?"

"Yes..."

"Simple and distinct...never answer if you're not alone...just say it's a reminder on your calendar. Always erase the contact immediately. I am leaving early tomorrow. After midnight, you won't be able to reach me. Tell Mimi I stopped by to get information about your husband's co-workers, nothing more. From here on out, that's all she needs to know. She's just a dumb kid and she needs to stay out of grown folks business. You need to trust me on this, lady. If you start talking to people, you might never see your husband alive again. Keep your mouth shut..."

"I will," she said, rising from the fluffy sofa. She offered me her hand and I shook it, very business-like. She held it longer than she needed to...the play was smooth but obviously well-practiced. "Be careful there, in Costa Rica, very careful. If you need to talk to me again…tonight perhaps, before you leave…"

"No, thank you," I said.

It's one thing to curry favor, another thing to play with fire.

CHAPTER 8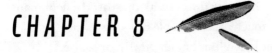

Ze'ev wanted a meeting of the minds. We decided to make it a send-off as well. I told Charity Fields to make it all happen, but to arrive later than Ze'ev and I.

Harvelle's Jazz Club was long and thin and wondrously dim… lots of history, and plenty of steamy atmosphere. The stage sat far back, to the rear. A brilliant jazz guitarist with a soft, gravelly voice was doing his thing, and the place was not nearly as loud or raucous as on most other nights.

I had not seen Ze'ev so focused and driven in a long, long time.

"As you know, Phillip, it rarely happens this way…a sweet development nonetheless, all because you took on the Sabo case. You really shook the branches and rattled the leaves today. I had no idea we'd hit the jackpot this afternoon…the young one could lead us straight to the hornet's nest."

"That Iranian kid? I don't know, Ze'ev."

"Why the doubt?"

"I don't like jumping the gun." I took a sip of Arack and water on ice, an Old World drink in an elegant blue bottle which Ze'ev had somehow smuggled into Harvelle's. The place almost personified darkness; that may have helped.

"Jumping the gun? Explain…"

"He could be a link," I said. "Or he could be a plant. He might just be talking out of his sphincter…that's the problem, you never know." I took a sniff of the Arack and gazed at its pale murkiness. It looked clear in the blue bottle, but had emulsified upon contact with water. Made in Lebanon…strange stuff. "How'd you sneak this past the door man? These places are always touchy about people bringing in their own."

"I didn't sneak it in. I paid him off. Discreetly, of course."

"Oh… I'll keep that in mind."

"Do you like it?"

"The Arack? No…" I smiled politely to ease the hurt—"Sorry chum. It's certainly different…but too strong. What is it, rubbing alcohol or cheap Kailua?"

"Ouch," Ze'ev said, slightly miffed. "It's quite a popular cocktail mixer in Tel Aviv, you know…"

"It's bottled in Beirut, Ze'ev. Maybe there's a reason they ship it to Tel Aviv."

"Hmm…where I'm from it is called Lion's Milk," Ze'ev said. "It's a test of your manhood—I'm so disappointed you find it unsavory…"

The drink was not my main concern.

I have always been skeptical of 'facts' gathered from people under duress. According to Ze'ev, young Hamid Safi threw his father under the bus at the first mention of Guantánamo and kept talking long after he stopped giving useful information.

"Ze'ev, listen. I don't get too excited about this type of news. No need to waste time lecturing one another, we both know that. Just keep in mind that we already know terrorists are hiding out in Central America, ever since the days of 'Shock and Awe,' half an eternity ago."

"Phillip…"

"Let me finish…we know that Hezbollah operatives routinely trade weapons and money for access to the trade routes and secret tricks of the drug cartels. The cartels are masters at avoiding detection. That expertise certainly comes in handy for smuggling people as well, we know all that. What we don't know is exactly who or what is infiltrating our borders, what level of threat they impose. That's Anti-Terrorism 101."

"That's all true," said Ze'ev. "However, Hamid Safi provided remarkably accurate information regarding "*Vespula*.""

"*Vespula*... that Hezbollah agent you've tracked for the past few years. Brazil, Honduras, El Banco Puro... *Vespula* can't be his real name, by the way, if he comes from Iran or Lebanon."

"No one knows his actual identity. I've spent almost two decades tracking him. They made me back off when I was active. Now, I'm free to do as I wish. Don't bother telling me I'm obsessed. I already know. We scared the Iranian boy, true, but he is still useful to both of us."

"You have not convinced me. That's all I am saying…"

"He knew travel patterns, known behaviors, collateral contacts, and probably most important, names," said Ze'ev. "His father, Maziar Safi, is helping establish Hezbollah cells in San Antonio Texas, Los Angeles, and Phoenix. The FBI knows that now. They are moving on that information as we speak. According to the boy, his father reports directly to *Vespula*. All payments to his father were made through El Banco Puro…that's where Safi kept all his money."

I had to admit that tidbit sounded compelling.

"I'm starting to think that El Banco Puro was the financial hub of cartel activity and terrorist planning throughout Central America," I said.

"Now you're using that thinking cap you shelved for six months," said Ze'ev. "Well, here's something that should interest you a bit more. The Safi kid led the Feds straight to his father's hotel room…the Jolly Roger in Marina Del Rey. They called me, and I met them there. We found his El Banco Puro financial records…two different accounts, one small, one large. On paper he was a millionaire…periodic payments in the thousands…most electronic, but one huge deposit of five-hundred-thousand cash on the same date I spotted *Vespula* stopping at the bank. Jackpot."

"Indeed…"

"We also found a cell phone with a series of messages, all in code. The phone was old man Safi's—at least that's what the son claimed.

Now, get this…a few days ago my Mossad connection in *San Jose* intercepted several texts from *Vespula* to that very same phone. Most of the texts were numerical, but one simply demanded the missing money in the most undiplomatic terms. Safi was scared…that's why he wanted Mimi Sabo, for leverage, to get to her father before he took the fall for all that money. It seems the Safi's were money handlers…money movers…facilitators providing cover."

"Obviously…"

"And by the way, Maziar Safi recently invested money into a small industrial plant in Santa Ana, CA called *Agua-Azul.* They manufacture water treatment equipment, water-bottle making machinery, and liquid storage tanks."

"Yikes. That's not reassuring," I said. "You mentioned numerical texts… numbers. What kind of numbers? Money, bank accounts, secret codes…what?"

"Simple math problems. Perhaps a dozen of them. Things like, 0.25 times 6.456… 1.75 times 5.22… 2.87 times 14.59, over and over. It took me a while to figure it out, I had almost forgotten. I think the Feds are still punching those numbers into their computer, Phillip."

"They are wasting their time," I said. "All they need is pencil and paper…"

We had worked together eight years earlier, in Honduras, a kidnapping case. The constantly moving kidnappers had devised a code to inform accomplices of the location of their captive. A list of number pairs, multiplied together, would be sent in sequence. Alone, the numbers meant nothing. The mathematics meant nothing. Only when the first factors were added together, and then the second factors were added together would the numbers have meaning. The code's structure was simple, in itself, merely a time waster for the uninitiated. "What did you come up with, Ze'ev?"

"9.866368 times 84.049096… that's quite a pair, wouldn't you say?"

Long story short, the final sums were merely geographic coordinates,

North and South, the only difference being that with the advent of GPS devices, the exact location could be decimalized, further complicating the ruse.

"Some place south...perhaps where I'm headed?"

"Of course...the coordinates mark the outskirts of a huge shanty town in *San Jose*, Costa Rica, known as *Los Guido*."

"Interesting... anything else?"

"Oh yes, I'm full of intrigue and bolts from the blue tonight."

"Like the Arack in the pretty blue bottle," I quipped.

"Well said. Now hear this...a disturbance took place in the shanty town a few days ago. Tenants were evicted from their shacks by members of Fuerzo *Publica*, supposedly to facilitate a narcotics investigation. A soft security perimeter has been established. However, my Mossad contact has photographed several men within the security perimeter dressed as police, but actually documented members of the North Valley Cartel...heavily armed...perhaps a dozen or more."

"Wow...that's excellent intelligence, Ze'ev. I didn't know you had it like that."

"There's more. That particular site lies in a part of the *Los Guido* shanty town known as *El Agujero*..."

"The hole..."

"Yes. It lies in a shallow basin...just one or two structures... a single inlet road—one way in, one way out. I believe there is a good chance, based on everything we know..." Ze'ev simply shrugged.

He did not have to finish.

My task had suddenly become quite daunting.

"If you like, I can arrange transportation for you, non-military, of course."

"It's my case Ze'ev, my mission. Mrs. Fields has already arranged my transportation, per my usual contacts. I will leave as planned, and contact your training center in *Limon*. I prefer *Limon*. From there I can move on *San Jose*."

"The cartels are always well armed. You might reconsider going alone…unless you have arranged 'collaborative assistance' on your own."

"If by collaborative assistance, you mean hired guns…I will do so if the situation calls for it. Nicaragua is just a stone's throw away. There are plenty of ex-soldiers there. It might come down to that…but as you know…"

"Yes…you prefer to work alone. But I must tell you friend…I will be there too, because now I know that *Vespula* is involved."

"If you don't mind me asking Ze'ev—and even if you do—why the hard-on for *Vespula*…"

Ze'ev Pinsky's eyes went dead cold.

CHAPTER 9

"1992…Buenos Aires…The Israeli embassy was bombed…twenty-nine innocents killed…still unsolved. My twin brother, T'zvi… lost a hand and was blinded. He was only visiting. He was a musician, Phillip, a good one… and a fine artist." Ze'ev sighed, wearily. "He was never the same after that. We were never the same, never again. The Iranians… there's no proof of it, but…they paid *Vespula* to blow up that embassy. I know it."

"I'm sorry, Ze'ev."

"So am I… *Vespula* did it. He is Hezbollah, and Hezbollah is supported by Iran. Two years later, same city, different bomb…a Jewish community center blown to bits, and another eighty-five people killed… still unsolved after all these years. *Vespula* was there, too. He was recently arrested in Bolivia with explosive devices. Bolivian officials let him go, despite an Interpol warrant for his arrest. Bastards! I assure you, I will not let him go…"

We sat and listened to the blues man on stage at the other end of Harvelle's. He started singing John Lee Hooker's 'Stripped Me Naked' and the guitar cried the way it needed to, in all the right places. I knew Ze'ev was crying on the inside, too. I brooded, and took a tiny sip of the Arack. It wasn't so bad…I might even learn to like it.

"Well, well, hello gentleman…" Charity Fields had arrived, in a snug fitting black jumpsuit that complimented her perfectly. Her blond hair was up, and she wore some nice jewelry on her wrist and throat, yet somehow she still looked quite professional. Ze'ev's eyes brightened a bit. A waitress walked by and Charity paused her with a quick flurry of her fingers, "Hi Jillian, a Blues Buster when you get a chance, please?"

"Ah, Ms. Charity Fields..." chimed Ze'ev. "Perfect timing to lift a weary heart. But shouldn't you be home with your young prince?"

"He's with grandpa for now. Boy's night in... So here I am, all glammed, playing the part... Hi Boss, is there room for three?"

"We'll make room," I said.

She had instantly brightened our little section of Harvelle's. Yet inside, I felt strangely anxious and tense, all at once. It felt as though something or someone...unseen...had touched my thoughts, yet been drowned out by everything around me and everything in my head...there was simply no way I could focus and reel it in. I heard my two companions speaking cheerily, but not really. Something else had whispered on the wind. I had lost it, and now my mind would not rest peacefully...

"Boss..."

"...What?"

"I was just saying... We can't stay out too late. We have a big day ahead of us tomorrow, don't we?"

"We..." I said. "Big day? What's that supposed to mean, Mrs. Fields?" I sounded distracted, even to myself.

She looked at Ze'ev. "Nothing, sir. I meant 'we' as in us...the team...you, sir...'big day' as in you're leaving tomorrow. Are you okay, sir?"

She only used 'sir' when something was wrong. I knew exactly what she had meant, but had allowed that strange feeling to get the better of me. I looked at the glass of Arack, then at Ze'ev...No, don't go there. It was not the alcohol; it was something else inside my head. I struck a conciliatory tone. "Actually, it might be better if I get a little rest, Charity."

"I just got here, sir...You can't leave me alone with Mr. Pinsky." They both laughed gently, and I smiled appropriately.

"I know I shouldn't, but...just put everything on my tab. Ze'ev, Charity... I need to meditate...to rest...to say good-bye to my son... please have a good time. Ze'ev... behave."

"I will call you, tomorrow," said Charity. "First thing..."

"Do you have your cell phone on?" asked Ze'ev. I nodded, and rose from the table. "Good," he said. "Keep it on, so I can keep track of you...be safe."

I exited Harvelle's and turned right, passing a smoke shop. Inside, I saw a handsome man and a pretty, petite woman. She wore a fine mink stole and we made friendly eye contact. I then turned up into the parking structure next to the smoke shop. I was parked on the second level, which was well-lit. As I made my way to the Ferrari, I heard the sound of footsteps and laughter and looked back. It was the young woman in the mink stole, escorted by the man in the shop. She looked happy. In fact, they were both in very good spirits. I heard her mention the name of the blues singer at Harvelle's and I heard him tell her that they would have to come back again on Burlesque Night, and then another burst of exuberant laughter echoed through the garage. As I pulled my keys from my pocket and prepared to remotely unlock the vehicle, I looked back once more. They were closer, and the woman had just removed her mink stole. The handsome man hugged her shoulder and she smiled warmly at him. She seemed to revel in his touch. She saw me looking and said, "Did you like the show?"

"Yes I did," I said, "Very"—and in that instant, she threw the stole across my face...a perfect toss, I must confess. It billowed open and enveloped my head, blinding me, and the man moved in swiftly and stuck an object against my body. I felt a sudden, incredible shock...and never felt myself hit the ground. I was helpless...unable to respond.

"Hurry...his hands, his hands, *his hands!*"

Through the fog I felt a needle prick me at the base of my neck... then felt nothing more.

CHAPTER 10

Everyone cracks eventually. That's my thinking. You can play the tough guy for only so long.

In fact, some deviant types actually enjoy your gallant efforts, so they can get their jollies breaking you down. My main captor, the 'mink lady,' seemed of that stripe. In the hands of real-life ogres like her, it's usually best to 'crack' a little and string them along if you can. If you play it right you'll live longer. Even if the pain makes you regret your reprieve, hang on.

If you're alive, there's always hope.

...The oblong room was warm, and dark in the shadowy corners. I 'came to' suddenly, like an old junkie from a soft nod.

"What the hell is this," I grumbled.

"Strike One, for you..."

My whole body convulsed when an ice-riddled bucketful of cold slush slammed into my face. It was the classic rude awakening from every dime store novel ever written—but damn effective nonetheless. My ears rang, my eyes blazed, and my head throbbed like a bass drum in a military parade.

I heard a metal bucket drop to the floor with a loud crash.

"I trust you slept well..."

It was 'mink lady,' from the parking structure. I felt sure of it. Her voice bounced softly off the walls... metal walls, gauging from the reverb. I lowered my torso and shook my head, letting the water drip

away, feigning more grogginess than I felt. They had strapped me to
a chair, apparently one designed for that very purpose. My watch had
been removed, as well as my shirt. My slacks and shoes remained. I had
no idea how long I had been down.

"Where am I?"

If I had thought anyone would actually answer, I might have raised
my head.

"My cruel world," her voice said, chillingly. "Welcome…and now
tell me who you work for." Her tone lacked any pretense of curiosity…
so I figured she already knew or thought she knew.

"Please, I'm just a software salesman and a part-time actor…"

That didn't go over well. I heard her hiss and snap her fingers.
Someone moved and I thought for sure that I would get shot in the back
of the head, just like that. Instead, another cascade of icy slush ripped
into my back, and another empty bucket clanged across the floor.

A burst of laughter erupted. I knew then that three men were
standing close by.

"Save that for the usual fools…that's Strike Two."

"May I lift my head?"

"Of course…"

I squinted and grimaced to express my discomfort—not that it
took much acting. She smiled, apparently pleased with herself. She
would be my Grand Inquisitor, it seemed. She stood at the table that
separated us, lording over my personal belongings, including my dis-
mantled cell phone. Thankfully, my precious black-faced ESQ watch
lay intact next to my wallet. No doubt, they had gone through everything, or so they thought. She had removed the makeup she wore in
the parking structure, and I realized that she had truly piled it on. Her
face looked remarkably plain now, a stark change from the mink-toting
vixen who orchestrated my downfall. Two men in black battle fatigues
stood behind her, leaning on the wall and cradling Mexican-made
Mendoza HM3 submachine guns. A third man, unarmed, kept watch
at a sliding door which was cracked open to ventilate his smoldering

cigarette. A single low-watt bulb dangled from the ceiling, casting strange shadows everywhere.

I suddenly realized we were inside an old, renovated boxcar, like the troop movers from the 1940's. I couldn't tell if we sat on rails or just plain ground.

"Listen," I said, letting my voice crack—in my best fearful tone, "I don't know who you are, or if you'll believe me, but I am not an agent or a spy or anything like that. I'm just a private citizen. A girl asked me to help find her father. He's a banker and he's been kidnapped. She offered me a few thousand bucks, and I took it because I'm broke. I only wanted to help. I'm not Derek Flint or James Bond, for God's sake. The car you saw me driving…it's not even mine…you probably already know that. I'll tell you whatever you want to know. This was all one big mistake…"

"You are right on two counts. One, you made a big mistake… and two, you don't know who I am. You're about to find out though…" She snapped her finger again and the smoker standing at the boxcar's sliding door flicked away his cigarette. He moved to her side, carrying a large, square object he had paused to retrieve from the shadows. It was covered with a fitted fabric. He placed the covered box onto the table, and then bent down and lifted a third silvery pail from the floor. I heard the slush settle as the pail dropped onto the tabletop, and watched rivulets of condensed water dribble down its outer surface.

She removed the fabric which covered the box and revealed a transparent cube enclosure. Inside, lots of one-inch ants milled about restlessly, carpeting the bottom of the cube and jostling for room on bamboo strips littering the interior. It may have been dozens…or… perhaps hundreds. Knowing what I knew, things did not look good for me. They were not fire ants, or Amazonian army ants—I would have preferred them, given a choice…

"Let me introduce you to my little friends," she said warmly,

"Conga Ants," I whispered. Damn…game over.

"Yes… *Paraponera clavatas.* I guarantee, when they are through with you, you will beg me to splash you with this icy water...then we will really talk, if you haven't screamed apart your own vocal cords." She smiled again. It made me want to make an ugly face at her, but it was no time for antagonism.

She was not exaggerating...and somehow I knew she was not bluffing. Paraponera clavatas... the words sent chills down my spine.

Conga Ants...cruel little devils roaming the moist jungles of Central America like stoic, wingless wasps, their stings shooting a neurotoxin twenty times stronger than any hornet...chemical fire.

Imagine big, red-hot needles piercing your skin, never cooling, and never going away... for hours.

I braced myself. She actually used her bare fingers to pluck the first specimen from the cube. "They are actually quite docile, until aggravated." She held it up and blew upon it and then came around the table and stood at my shoulder. "They don't like the smell of mammal breath...or body odor." She waved it around my shoulder near the armpit. "That excites them... and the poison has evolved to devastate smooth muscle tissue... like the flesh of your trapezius." She dropped it on my shoulder.

"Hmmmpph!!" The sheer pain was indescribable...and instantaneous!

I literally screamed with my mouth closed, if one can imagine such a thing—and that was just the first one.

The burning...it would not go away...would not subside...refused to fade...no matter how much I squirmed or twisted... and as I settled into a concentrated breathing pattern, controlling it somewhat with my mind...she dropped another...then dropped another...and another... and yet another...choice spots, tender intimate spaces...countless times, all punctuated by innumerable yelps and bloody-painful screams...deep breathing, to no damn avail! I imagine I looked like a savage werewolf to them, with my sweat and spittle flying everywhere...and as the men laughed and hooted with relish, spastic, crazy, seizure-like shudders came over me...and then a mad, uncontrollably fast trembling...

Then she placed one in the crease of my ear... and another at the apex of one breast...then the other...

"Aaaarrrrggh!!" I actually bit my own tongue and tasted my blood, that's how bad it hurt... I thought I would start sobbing uncontrollably... at that point I really didn't care. Then, finally, the icy water slammed into me with tremendous force...and yes it hurt, but by God, right then I felt damn grateful. One of the men brought in a nozzled hose, and moved in to spray me down. The jet of water struck too harshly and I yelped miserably.

"No, you fool!" She snatched the hose from him, then gave it back. "Remove this nozzle, imbecile! Then go get another bucket of ice!"

Then the water came soft, and gentle. She poured it delicately upon my head and body... "I think you are ready...yes?" I nodded in utter defeat and she cooed, as if the others were not even there, "I'm so proud of you..."

"Yeah, I'll bet." I had never felt such agonizing pain in my life...as if I had charged a fire-breathing dragon, and lost decisively.

"They made me do it...You are my strong, sexy man now..."

"Not now, Sweety," I muttered, "I'm dying here..." Her mind game was crude.

"No...you are mine now. I won't hurt you anymore...I promise..."

I wondered if that included her poorly-spun reverse psychology... She was actually not all that bad. She had the voice for it, if not the looks.

"Okay," she said softly, after the water went away. "We'll talk now. Don't lie to them, or they will kill you. I want you to live, so tell the truth... Where is Juan Miguel Sabo being held?"

"In Costa Rica...the exact location... I wish to God I knew. I think in *Limon*, or perhaps another town. That is why the girl offered me money, to find him."

"Why *Limon*?"

She took the bait. She should have pressed for the location again...

"Because I don't think he was kidnapped." Utter rubbish!

"What do you mean? It's all over the news..."

"I think he went into hiding, and plans to escape the country."

She turned and looked at the man who had stood watch at the door. They said nothing, and then she turned back to me. She looked me very deeply in my eyes.

"Why *Limon*...tell them."

I had to somehow keep talking. Delay, delay, delay...

"*Limon* has a sea port and that's how he's planning to leave...by sea. All the money is in a bank in the Cook Islands. The CIA helped him and now they're trying to get him out of the country, so they can get paid. All the airports are being watched. But not the port of *Limon*..."

"How do you know all this?"

"I'm a former Federal Agent."

"What department."

"Defense Investigative Services. Back then my name was Charles Peterson. After 9-11, DIS merged with FBI, but some of us went to CIA. I worked there for three years out of the Miami branch office. Check it out if you like. My bosses smuggled Cuban embezzlers away from Havana and gave them new identities in America in exchange for millions. I wouldn't play ball, so they burned me out. I still have friends in the CIA, though... one of them told me that's what is going down with Juan Sabo."

"If that is true, then why go to Costa Rica?"

"For the money his daughter promised me. He's got everybody fooled. My military and Homeland Security contacts are insistent that there's been no kidnapping. I took the girl's money, so I have to make a show of following through. I planned on going there and after Sabo got out, say I rescued him and helped him escape. It's all a big secret, so how would his daughter know otherwise? That's all...I just wanted a few bucks. My CIA friend thinks he knows where he is…" More bait… more reason to talk. More time on the books.

For a while I held their rapt attention. By then I had surmised that they all worked for somebody else who had lost a ton of money in Juan Sabo's scheme. So, I rambled on about intercepted radio transmissions, secret money transfers, messages I received from my CIA friends and various escape routes involving the Costa Rican Coast Guard. I owed a lot of that gibberish to my prior Costa Rica gig, so I sounded convincing, minus any real scrutiny. "…The first place I plan to look—if you let me leave here—is in the secret tunnels dug beneath the *Tortuguero* Canals, just north of the Port of *Limon*…"

I knew they would never let me out of there alive. But they were willing to be delayed by my tales of intrigue.

What they didn't know was that I was also keeping one eye on my black-faced, ESQ watch lying on the table in front of me. A small blue diode along its side, facing me, had begun to blink, a flash so tiny you wouldn't notice it unless you knew to look for it, and even then you might not fathom its purpose. For me, it meant that Ze'ev Pinsky had locked onto my GPS coordinates. Now I had hope.

So I kept rambling, but eventually the lookout man grew restless. He walked over to the table and started looking at my things. I saw his eyes admiring the watch. I kept talking, as he picked it up. He began turning it over in his hands, probably deciding that he would keep it after he had blown my brains out.

Then he saw the blinking diode. He smiled at first, as if it were a curiosity, and touched the diode with his finger. Then he shook the watch at his ear and looked it over again. I kept talking, kept talking… and talking. The man looked at me, then the watch, and finally me again. I wondered if he suspected that a blue diode had no business on such an older watch, or that the light kept blinking faster as time went on. He seemed preoccupied by it…fascinated…or suspicious. Then the watch began emitting a tiny beeping sound, like an auditory beacon. He stared, brooding…and finally, somehow he just knew.

"This is all lies!" He slung the watch at my chest. The woman turned to him, confused, and he slapped her face so hard that she fell to the floor, "He's playing you!" The lookout man spun toward one of his *compadres* and shouted, "Shoot!"

The gunman raised the submachine gun and pointed at my chest. I was dead. My gambit had failed…

"Not him, her," ordered the lookout man, now turned angry leader. "Now!"

"No!" the woman screamed, rising and raising her hands in protest. A burst of rapid gunfire silenced her and literally pinned her to the floor. Her ploy had failed, and she paid the ultimate penalty… her life. She had never been calling the shots.

"Now shoot this lying *mosca*," ordered the new boss, pointing at me.

Damn… I was dead all over again.

Ever the survivor, I flung my whole body to the left, and crashed to the hard floor in a chair-bound heap. In my panic, I forgot I had all those ant stings until I hit the floor. Then it all came back to me, and the burning, living hell re-intensified. But it didn't matter, because I was done for. The table offered no cover, and his poor angle could easily be rectified…if only I could find a third degree of separation…but too late…my killer had already shifted on his feet, adjusted and swooped in, barrel first.

A short burst of gunfire roared— but from the doorway. My would-be assassin lifted off the floor and crumpled like an old brick chimney, without pulling off a single shot. Ze'ev Pinsky then swiftly pivoted and drew down on the second gunner with his KRISS Super V…it looked mighty mean and could spit out .45-caliber slugs with no recoil —one reason it is the best submachine gun in the world.

"Party's over, amigo," growled Ze'ev. "Put it down." The gunner made his move anyway, so Ze'ev let him have it, waist high and rising as the steel ripped him through. "…Lights out in London." Ze'ev now had the last man standing under threat of fire. "Phillip, are you okay?"

"I'll live."

"Good." Without hesitation Ze'ev advanced on the lookout man. He kicked him squarely in the *cajones*, elbowed his jaw, and then clubbed him hard on the head… a not-very-nuanced attack that proved effective and established the new pecking order. "This one we take alive… Charity! Get in here!" My secretary entered and rushed to my side.

She began un-strapping me. "Oh God, sir…" She sounded distressed.

"Quit calling me 'sir', Charity. What are you doing here?"

"Ze'ev needed transportation. The Tesla would never get you guys back…no juice."

"I need a doctor Ze'ev."

"Yes I know, but first things first…" He kept the KRISS Super V trained on the last man, now in plasti-cuffs and seated with his back against the wall…Ze'ev walked over to examine the Conga Ants. "These little guys ain't nothing nice." He carried the container back to his captive and placed it on the floor next to him. Then he pointed his weapon directly at the man's head. "Close your eyes, amigo." The man complied. "Nice…now open them again…That's what it means to be alive. Do you like that feeling?" The man nodded slowly. "Good. Who do you work for…"

"*Vespula*…I do not know him…I have a family."

By that time Charity had freed me and I painfully managed to sit up straight. The man with the gun to his head had begun to cry.

"We all have family, amigo," said Ze'ev.

"Dr. Temple, Ze'ev…get me to him…quick and in a hurry."

CHAPTER 11

What a difference a half-day makes...

I sat securely strapped in my soft leather seat feeling rather relaxed, despite my earlier ordeal. Over time, the helicopter's powerful drone even became hypnotic. I was impressed that Charity had come through once again.

Now, if anyone had suggested twenty-four hours earlier that I would be flying along Nicaragua's southern Pacific coast in an A119 Koala, I would have bet a wad of cash against it. If they had predicted everything else that went down, I would have wagered my Z4 and a full tank of gas that they were dreaming.

Still, there I sat... zooming along, one thousand feet above sea level and looking out my window at all the nice scenery. How chipper... Actually, I counted myself lucky not to be plugged full of holes. If that weren't enough, I was flying straight into what might be the most dangerous mission of my life. How chipper, indeed...

"Below us to the left is the Nicaragua resort town I mentioned earlier," piped in my pilot, from the cockpit. "San Juan del Sur...look at that coastline."

"Nice. Drop her down some if you can... it's beautiful." I wasn't expecting a high-speed, low-level pass, but she swooped the big bird down with an exhilarating rush of power and flew parallel to the coast-line with the fuselage slightly tilted, so I could take it all in.

"Good stuff," said the pilot.

"Yeah, it doesn't matter how many times I see the Pacific coastline from up high," I said. "It's always a thrill."

"Yes, same here... You see that alcove...that one right over there... they film some reality show down there. They might be doing one right now."

Yeah?" I chuckled. "Maybe we ought to drop in on 'em...the place seems more like paradise than purgatory to me."

"Yeah, right... buzz the tropical campers and then off we go? Piss off the Nicaraguan Air Force...nice."

The helicopter swung hard east and left San Juan del Sur behind. In less than an hour I would hit the ground near *Limon*, but in the meantime I tried to unwind and take in all the scenery. My mind drifted back to the night before, in the basement laboratory of Dr. Brownell Temple, the black ex-CIA doctor who treated my injuries.

When we arrived, I had started having convulsions from so many ant stings. He put me down again right away but it seemed only briefly, like I had slept for just an hour or two, and I felt pretty good when I woke. The good doctor had worked wonders in a very short time, I thought. Boy, was I mistaken.

———————

"*...According to this blood test, brother man, your captors put you down with Diprivan...*"

"*Why have I heard of that drug before...*"

"*It's generic for Propofol...a white liquid anesthesia...fast acting, and quickly metabolized, therefore relatively safe. It's the stuff that killed Michael Jackson, you know, but whoever did you dirty apparently knew exactly what they were doing. You won't have any bad side effects at all. Obviously it didn't stop your heart, right? You seemed completely unaffected by the Diprivan when you first arrived...but the ant venom had begun doing a real number on you. Too many stings.*"

"*The Diprivan...no harm?*"

"None."

"Temple…are you sure?"

"Come on, Phillip… I'm a doctor and a former CIA interrogation specialist. I have shot Diprivan into people countless times, and stronger meds as well. For normal surgical purposes, Diprivan works like a charm. Maybe that's why rich cats like MJ paid so handsomely for it… Three hours down is like getting eight hours of really good sleep. In fact, if they had not tortured you, you might have woken up feeling better than you have in a long time. Of course, slush showers and Conga Ants are not my notion of ideal counter-treatments."

Temple had that way about him, a brilliant store of medical and physiological knowledge coupled with a wry humor that only life in 'The Company' would foster in a man. He had retired from the CIA a few years earlier and broken off all ties. No one who really knew why ever really said why. He then turned his house into a 'toy shop' and made specialty devices for guys like Ze'ev and myself. He refashioned the ESQ watch I wore that night, so indirectly he had already saved my life.

"The pain from the stings is completely gone, Temple… how?"

"Were you that far gone, or did you just forget everything? Wow. Well, first I provided a mild sedative and an anesthetic—plus a double shot of tequila because I'm the doctor, then electro-shocks individually administered to each sting site. Afterwards, you slept for twelve hours…it's four o'clock in the afternoon, my man."

"You're—"

"Kidding? How cliché that sounds, and so incorrect. Mrs. Fields and Mr. Pinsky stayed until noon…then both left."

"Where to?"

"Ze'ev? You know him. Off on another rampage or some clandestine information hunt. He mentioned something about a man being stuffed in the trunk of Mrs. Fields' car, and having to take him somewhere…I think the fellow was still alive, because he asked me if I had any truth serum. That man…he's really quite a deadly character…but I and Mrs. Fields wanted no part of that."

"*Where is she?*"

"*Took my car...borrowed it, to be returned in one piece, she said. She'll be back, soon. She is out following your standing orders, Phillip. That means arranging your travel to Costa Rica...She may be in completely over her head right now, thanks to you.*"

"*Don't underestimate Mrs. Fields. I don't anymore.*"

"*Believe me... I never underestimate anyone. She's quite loyal too... it's a shame she doesn't work for me. I was like that once...young and gung-ho to play follow the leader. I'm against all this current activity, Phillip. I don't think you should go. You need more time to recover...It's too much too soon, but I realize I'm talking to a deaf man...*"

"*Yeah, you are, but at least you're smart enough to know it. It's hard to believe that I lost half a day... and that electrical shots could end pain like that.*"

"*The shocks did more than end the pain. They neutralized the poison and, stopped its spread throughout your system...killed all its effects. You were stung thirty-nine times. That's a lot of venom.*"

"*Temple...you're simply a genius, that's all.*"

"*I wish I was, my brother. I am brilliant to be sure, but certainly no genius. I did not invent the technique. Some say it started in the Amazon twenty years ago... people using stun guns. Others say it was the Texans, with car batteries and jumper cables for rattle snake bites. I only know it works. For you, I used a modified Taser. It delivers a near-perfect high-voltage, low-current shock.*"

"*That's it...?*"

"*Yes, that's it. One major drawback, though...each shock is quite painful, which is why I put you asleep beforehand. It was somewhat risky, given all you endured, but necessary because you were exhibiting a strong allergic reaction to the Conga Ant venom by the time you reached me.*"

"*Yes... I remember, now. The shakes ...then the spasms.*"

"*Exactly. I had to work fast. The technique is not textbook approved, but I have perfected it over the years to counteract various insect and scorpion stings...and venomous snake bites. I'm not going to bore you with the physiological details. No one truly knows why it works. You just need to know that neurotoxins effect the synapses and nerves and that electrical charges neutralize their deadly effects almost instantly. You'll be fine. By the way, Phillip, you have an incredibly low heart rate, and that may have slowed the venom's effects. Oh, and how's Malcolm these days? Still want to be a doctor, or was I just the flavor of the month back then?*

"Yeah, I'm afraid you were…"

"No problem, my man. As I recall he wanted to be a train conductor, a teacher, a bus driver and a vet during that same time frame…and in rapid succession. Six-year-olds…fickle souls… time flies, doesn't it?"

"Yes. And now you freelance, Temple."

"Yes I do, like you, just selling a different expertise. Although I must say…my new gig is ideal for where I'm at right now…your field of endeavor is a younger man's game. I could just never keep up now and I'm not sure how you still do it."

"I need to get up."

"You're quite free to move about now. There's food to eat…if you need anything else, don't hesitate. Later I will show you some of the things I have been working on. You might see something useful. I hope so, because as much as I object to your plans, I actually wish you well in Costa Rica, you adventurous fool…"

———

Before I departed, Temple had repaired my ESQ watch and reconfigured my cell phone to operate on an encrypted satellite signal. He also provided a rundown of current CIA activity in Central America, and everything he could gather about the Sabo case from personal contacts. That information included PDF dossiers on *Aguilera* and *Vespula*. We both wondered if they were somehow linked, but nothing concrete supported our thoughts…

…The A119 Koala landed on a farm near a small hub town called *Moin*, just four miles east of *Limon*. My pilot bid farewell with a sharp nod and a gloved 'thumbs up' for good measure. I carried a few things in a beat up old backpack and trekked north from the small farm to the main road that ran eastward to *Limon*. I looked up and saw a large green bird with a bright red breast and a long scissor tail flying overhead…I knew what it was but could not recall the name just then. I refocused and took a good look around. *Moin* had seemed more like a big stockyard than an actual town from the helicopter. On the ground, my opinion changed little. Fuel storage tanks, brick warehouses and a Dole Fruits train depot dominated the landscape. The air smelled of petroleum and the place felt dull…not exactly a tropical getaway, that's for sure. Once I got my land legs back I made good time despite the moist heat and hit the outskirts of *Limon* soon enough.

The first thing that stood out in *Limon* was the black population. Most were native born, of course, the ancestors of imported slave labor, but there were far greater numbers than I had a right to expect. In fact, a few looked like tourists from Belize or Haiti. Temple had mentioned something about a weeklong cultural fair, an annual event occurring across Costa Rica. I saw lots of posters, some promoting '*Limon* Roots,' others promoting *Flores De La Diáspora Africanas*. I stopped to read one and got the gist of it. It was Costa Rica's black history week. Perfect cover for my presence, I thought, and bought a T-shirt from the first street vendor I saw. After all, the more I blended in the better.

I entered a little restaurant called *El Quetzal*, very Aztec-themed, but not too touristy. I ordered coffee and something forgettable from the menu, and glanced about the place. Next to a small pyramid-shaped salt shaker, I noticed a black matchbook decorated with a long-tailed, bright green bird. Of course, I had seen one flying overhead upon my arrival, and suddenly recalled its name… *Quetzal*… just like the restaurant. I liked the matchbook's design and kept it. After I left, an old flatbed Ford filled with recyclables slowed down and stopped right next to me. A woman dressed like a dumpster diver sat at the wheel. Everything about her looked common and dirty, except her eyes. They were the lightest brown. That was the one nice thing about her, but it didn't matter. She could have been Eva Longoria in stiletto heels and I would have still been wary. I had eaten my fill of troublesome women.

She wore a headscarf and a light shawl and when she smiled, it lacked warmth—and that suited me fine. She motioned toward me to get into the truck. "Everybody likes *El Quetzal*. Hop in …"

Yeah right… I studied that face again. She was no junk collector.

"Who do you work for?" I asked. I put it to her in Spanish, too. *"Para quien trabajas?"*

She seemed a little surprised at my caution, but stepped out from the pickup and showed both hands. "No tricks here, amigo. Ze'ev asked me to make contact, that's all. He said you would turn me down, too…"

"Yeah?"

"Yeah. You're the big bad Kung Fu instructor, I hear. I'm nobody special, just your ride. Get in or keep walking. It's your choice…"

"Okay. Let's go…"

Neither of us spoke, and I kept waiting for an ambush that never occurred. When I arrived at the Pinsky School, I immediately went to the front desk, where I received a rather strange surprise.

"Ze'ev?" I could not believe he was actually sitting at the reception desk. He turned his head and regarded me through dark aviator sunglasses, but none of the usual warmth came through.

"I'm sorry. I think you have the wrong Pinsky. Ze'ev Pinsky is my brother. I'm T'zvi… T'zvi Pinsky, his twin. And you?" He extended his prosthetic right hand. I recovered quickly enough to shake it and spare us both any embarrassment.

"The pleasure is mine," I said. "I've worked with your brother Ze'ev from time to time. My name is Phillip."

"Oh…Phillip. My brother's sparring partner! Welcome."

CHAPTER 12

Under the dim glow of a small wax candle, her toned shoulders and smooth torso narrowed at the waist with astonishing grace, the elegant contours blending seamlessly with almost sinful perfection. I had not enjoyed such a passionate and energetic lover in some time, and I felt not just satisfied but mildly exuberant. Soon she murmured in the darkness, then sighed and shifted softly on the bed as her taut hips flexed and her luscious round bottom caught the light...and goodness gracious, once more I grew tensely aroused. Call it ardor or outright lust, but I couldn't help myself... I had to have her again, then and there. With customary assurance I placed my left hand upon her back... slid it down slowly, relishing the warm landscape...caressing, massaging... and gently clasping the firm, fleshy tush. She shivered, moaned quietly and arched her entire, sculpted derriere upward in response, then turned to face me with a curious gaze.

"...You're not?"

"Expended? Oh no, not hardly my sweet, not just yet..."

"No...? What about San Jose..."

"It will be there...Our delay is all your doing, Chava. There's no one else to blame....you're simply delectable...to see and to hold."

She scanned the length of my eager frame as I maneuvered to wrap her completely in my arms.

"You too, Phillip," she cooed, "...in more ways than one."

I made it my business to prove us both right, tapping out steady rhythms on her little drum kit until she erupted with a volcanic crashing of cymbals.

Earlier that morning, upon first arriving at Ze'ev's fighting school, I had absolutely no cause to believe my day would come to such a smashing conclusion. As fate would have it…it did.

T'zvi Pinsky certainly threw me for a loop shortly after our mutual introductions. Right away, someone came and ushered me off to the training and practice gym. The gym looked first class. A loudmouthed sensei-type had a dozen of the top kids going through their paces. I watched him a while. He was heavy on *his* form and *his* technique and a bit too pushy for my taste, and once or twice I saw him sizing me up out of the corner of his eye.

I recognized him for some reason but couldn't place him at first… it wasn't work-related, though.

Eventually, Ze'ev's brother T'zvi came to the gym with his guide dog and told them all I was a visiting master. The sensei guy frowned and coolly marched off to the free weights …apparently he resented the intrusion.

…Ah well, get over it.

I wasn't expecting a formal introduction but I warmed to the kids. I told them the history of Wing Chun Kung Fu and a few key concepts that I thought meshed well with their Krav Maga skills. T'zvi translated, which was convenient. The students stayed interested. They tried a few 'sticky hands' exercises, for tight spaces with no room to run. They liked it… I could tell that their main instructor didn't allow for much social interaction. They were highly disciplined…no spontaneity, very programmed…but good at what they did. One of them eventually asked me what I thought were the most important aspects of fighting …

"Interesting question," I said, through T'zvi Pinsky. "What are the most important things to all of *you?*"

They looked around a while until finally one said, *"Ataque y retírese."*

Classic Ze'ev-think. "Right...engage and disengage," I said. "Yeah. If you're not in the dojo, or at the gym, get in, do damage and get out *quick.* There's no sparring in the streets...no referee... remember that. Three seconds, three moves. Take him out and disengage. Just remember it's not all about the physical. It's also about awareness... outward awareness and inner awareness..."

"That's what they needed to hear, Phillip, all that."

We sat at the big long reception desk, where T'zvi spent much of his time. "We don't want them fighting on the corner, we want them gaining self-confidence. They don't get enough of the thinking part..."

"That's just the instructor's push," I said. "Speaking of which...who is he...what's his name?"

"Our instructor? He's new...Fields," said T'zvi Pinsky, rather flatly. "Baron Blaine Fields... That's his real name. He's only been here for a few weeks."

"Hmm," I said. "I know the face."

"From where?"

"Picture in an old album... he was married to my secretary, Charity, years ago. They had a kid, a boy...he's mildly autistic..."

"...And let me guess, he left her."

"Exactly, for the home-care giver...It all went down long before I met her. Still a mess. She stays with her folks now...nice gal, sharp, deserved better."

"We don't exactly adore him," said T'zvi. "Our real guy got called back to *Haifa*…security detail for the mayor, his uncle. Ze'ev says that Mr. Fields is here special request from Langley."

"Yeah? What for…eyes and ears?"

T'zvi snorted. "Hardly. It's not classified so I'll tell you what I know… if you even care to know."

I shrugged. "Shoot…"

"A stupid scandal blew up in Algiers. According to my brother the station chief there got in trouble for drugging and raping two Algerian women…I forget his name…a station chief! He filmed the attacks and stored images on his computer. Recalled…dismissed…a terrible blow."

"What about Fields?"

"He knew something but refused to cooperate with the Algerian authorities, which embarrassed the administration. So now this is Camp Washout for Fields."

"Interesting," I said, "I have a good mind to send for Charity. She always says she still owes him a punch in the nose…and what about you, T'zvi?"

"Me? Well…let's see…I started the Pinsky School to address the social issues affecting the kids here in *Limon*…the drugs, the gangs, the poverty, everything. It's so easy for some to close their eyes. Mine were closed…even when I could see they were closed. Now I'm blind but they're open, too. That's really what I'm all about, now, keeping good kids off the street so they don't go bad."

I liked T'zvi. He had a good heart, I could see that.

"Ze'ev told me you used to play the violin and Spanish guitar, as well." He nodded. I could see him remembering. I looked around at the school's interior walls. There were lots of paintings, the hyper-photorealistic kind that modern photography swept away long ago, the kind that still fascinates people who see it for the first time. "You painted everything on the walls, too?"

"Yes, a long, long time ago. Losing my sight and my good hand… it changed things, obviously"

"You were incredible."

"Yeah," said T'zvi. He sighed heavily. "Sometimes people still rave about them, the pictures I mean, but I've forgotten what most of them look like. Isn't that strange? It's a little frustrating too. It's like being a retired athlete, you know? People talk about the wonderful things you used to do—but you can't do those things anymore...I know what *that* feels like. But enough about me. Ze'ev keeps telling me that he wants you to help me run this place..."

That's not going to happen...Ze'ev knows that."

"Why not? We could use you, Phillip, and Costa Rica is like paradise..."

"Well, T'zvi... I'm a martial artist, but if I teach anything, it will be Wing Chun Kung Fu... exclusively." I thought a moment before speaking further. "I get into this with my son a lot, too, so don't take it wrong...but Krav Maga is really a mixed combat *style*—a good one, too. It's direct, it's tactical, it's brutal, it's efficient, and everything a fighting system should be. It's just not a true martial art."

"No?"

"No. It probably never will be, because it's too good at being what it is...a military fighting system. It's focused, but also limited in what I prefer to call its *spiritual usefulness.*"

"Hmm... I've never heard it put quite that way before, Phillip. I'm not sure what that means. It's practically the national fighting system of Israel. People everywhere love it..."

"Yes, of course, and it has a founder and a branching history and there are now undisputed masters of the style. But there's no enduring values, no life-defining customs, no holistic traditions involved. It's definitely more than just a sport, though. Put it this way T'zvi...Krav Maga is a way to preserve your life...but not a way to *live* your life."

"That's fine...that's fine." He cleared his throat with a soft little cough. "Ze'ev and his... colleagues here ...they have helped out from time to time..."

"That's probably not company policy, I bet," I said. "Not good for operational cover either..." I wondered if T'zvi understood my meaning.

Oh, *that.* I don't think Ze'ev even worries about it. Mossad? Is that what you meant by cover? My brother worked for them for so many years...it's beyond departmental loyalty and chains of command now. He's out of it, now. Completely."

"That's what I hear," I said, neutrally. But I also thought about Ze'ev's precise flow of intel, his intense hatred for *Vespula* and the utterly casual way he gunned down two hostiles the night before...without a moment's hesitation... He might've been out of the game, but he sure hit like he never left the playing field.

"T'zvi... a local woman picked me up today."

"Not exactly a local...just an excellent facsimile, I guess. It was the infamous *Chava Cresca*... one of ours."

"*Chava Cresca?* I like that. Is that her real name?"

"It's the one she answers to lately. I don't know what's real when it comes to names and identities anymore, Phillip... I'm not even sure who Ze'ev is from week to week...and he's my god dam brother!"

"Just curious..."

"You can ask her yourself...she's coming right now...I know that walk... drum your fingers if she's as fine as they all say..."

———

I heard the footsteps just then, and turned quickly to my right. A striking woman walked directly toward us with a head of wavy auburn hair... it bounced freely and brushed her shoulders gingerly with every springy step. She looked to be about forty, or maybe younger. It was hard to tell, with her tapered waste, agile-looking frame, pert upper torso and energetic legs that bloomed 'just so' at the upper thigh and filled her tan cargo pants perfectly.

To T'zvi's mild delight, I drummed my fingers lightly on his desktop, in unison with her crisp footfalls. "The kids got it right," *I said.* "She's fine as hell..."

She was a professional, no doubt about that. I spotted a slight bulge on her right ankle, just above her coffee-colored tactical boots...perhaps a light, polymer Jericho 941 handgun tucked away for a rainy day, standard issue for Israeli agents... and probably something with a lot more 'stoppage' concealed inside her cute beige duty vest. She was armed, dangerous and apparently quite comfortable in the role. I saw several other details at a glance, small little things...her left arm swung more freely than her right arm, unencumbered by the presence of any gun... her eyes scanned point to point, at a door, or a window, at the front main entrance. Eventually, those eyes bore in on me as she closed the final gap.

From the start, she had a way about her...

"*Chava Cresca,*" she said mildly, with a perfect accent. She stared at me long and hard. I felt a warm rush of attraction pass through me as we exchanged brief pleasantries. I casually stood and offered my hand. She extended her own and shook mine firmly, with no claim to dominance. Her palm was soft and warm, her fingers delicate, yet strong. She was even more attractive up close. The handshake lasted long enough for each of us to get our point across.

I studied her face closely... and suddenly it all came home to me... those big brown eyes were the give-away. She was the exact same woman who had transported me earlier, in the pickup truck...and she had tidied up very well...

"Miss Cresca, surely that wasn't you earlier today..." I said. "I found it hard to believe..."

"It was me," she said emphatically "Sorry for my scruffy appearance. I hope I look better now."

"I don't think there's any doubt about that," I said.

"Thank you..."

She smiled. It was a not a token gesture, but something more. I felt subtle electricity sparking from us every time our eyes met. Despite the formalities, she put something out there that I liked. She intrigued me… aroused my curiosity. She knew it, too. If sex appeal was her only weapon, Chava Cresca could have ditched the slingshot, and still slain Goliath like a champ.

"If you are up to it, we can recon The Hole in San Jose, as early as tonight. I'm' sure Ze'ev filled you in, but things always look different up close, right? In the meantime, I can show you your personal quarters if you like…You must be a little tired. Bring your things."

On that note, we left the reception area. I had a very warm feeling about Chava Cresca, but I couldn't exactly say why. She was hot, sure, and I liked it *plenty,* and I knew I couldn't trust her beyond a certain point, not blindly anyway. She was *Mossad, a*fter all. They had their own agenda… I was no fool about that. Her support had nothing to do with courtesy. She would play me like a fiddle if I let her and would probably help me only if it helped her, too. Still, all that was fine and dandy, though… I understood. I knew how the game was played, and I had an agenda of my own to fulfill. I definitely wanted more information from her but she didn't have to tell me anything if she didn't want to. …she was certainly no T'zvi Pinsky…she wouldn't spill beans just because I asked nicely—at least not at first. Despite all that, I still liked her.

"Ze'ev briefed me on *Mossad's p*urpose, here," I said, following her to the aft section of the building. "But he didn't tell me anything about you, in particular."

"I'm just your friendly neighborhood master spy…just observing to increase my knowledge base."

"Is that so?"

She nodded and opened a door which took us to another part of the building. Then she led me down a long corridor that ended at yet another door. She entered and I followed. It was a small studio sized room, decently equipped with a double bed, a study desk, and all the usual amenities of a hotel room. "This is your room. It's the only one down this corridor. You look like you could use a hot shower and some time to rest. Tonight we hit *San Jose*...to verify location...."

I couldn't argue with her thinking. I was feeling a little ripe and somewhat tired.

"Alright. I'm going to hit the shower, then..."

She made no move to leave, and just nodded at me.

"Feel free to stay," I said. It rang hollow to my own ears. I conceded her presence and left her to own devices. I took an extra-long hot shower. I knew Chava Cresca would go through all my things, anyway. It was standard practice. I didn't really care. She had a right to...it was her house. I would have done the same.

I expected her to still be there when I left the shower, but I didn't expect her to be standing there nude. I stood and gazed upon her, wearing nothing but a towel around my waist. She stood there too, facing me in all her golden glory, as pert and firm as I imagined when she came strutting up to me a few minutes before. All I could do was admire the view at first...she looked that good. Then my mind reactivated.

"Is this one of your master spy techniques?" I asked. "If it is, I surrender, but I can tell you right now, I hope to God it's not, because you're incredibly gorgeous."

She shook her head no, slowly, staring at me like a lonely goddess with golden-brown eyes. Daintily, she licked her pouty lips, swallowed, and spoke.

"I'm won't lie and say I've never done something like this before...I have"

"Good," I said. "I won't lie and say I haven't either."

I took the few steps necessary to draw near. I raised my hand carefully to her face and gently ran my fingers along her smooth jaw line. She turned her face upward and bit her lower lip, and it made my blood simmer.

"Earlier today" she whispered, "...I decided..." She stood on her tippy-toes, closed her eyes and softly pecked my lips, again and again, "that I simply had to...have you."

Her seductive brown eyes opened and like a skydiver rushing to earth I fell into them...fast and hellishly quick.

That was all she wrote.

In that same moment she was in my arms. Her tight body felt like a portion of paradise, bountiful and rich for the taking...her breasts swelled like ripening fruit in my agile hands, the tips on point and rigid. Everywhere I touched I felt warmth and flesh and an incredible exchange of sensual, hot desire...cosmic volts passing between us...my lips smothering hers, her tongue melting mine... slithering, slippery-moist kisses, hot and enticing, driving us to rare heights. My loins literally raged under her sultry ministrations. Then suddenly, with a playful growl she threw her arms about my neck and leapt up, wrapping her wonderful thighs around me, right where I stood.

Incredible...like a passionate farm girl forcing herself on the wiry hired help—and helpful I was, placing my hands beneath her for support, and taking her as she so willingly offered. I wanted to carry her to the waiting bed...but she had other plans...so as physically demanding as it was, I went along for as long it took to satisfy her. She moved like a woman too long deprived of good old-fashioned loving... and believe me; I had that in ample supply. She had me gasping for air when the thunder cracked for her, and I rode out the storm like a good ranger should. She howled and whimpered like a she-wolf as the bolts of lightning struck and then finally faded...then she clung to me and pulled me for grateful, deep kisses. It was all her show, but I was already contemplating the inevitable encore... as we kissed with the great big world spinning around us.

Sometimes, it's good to be The Specialist.

CHAPTER 13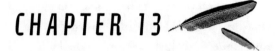

Life has its funny twists and turns... put me in a tough fix and I can outfight, out punch or out kick any three men I ever tangled with, yet in the end I'm still a sap for a damsel in distress...or a dog. I proved that for the umpteenth time while watching a parade in the center of *Limon* with Chava Cresca at my side...

Chava had left quietly after our thunderous lovemaking session, leaving me to recover both my strength and my senses, and later that day just after sunset, as I read the *Vespula* dossier, she called my room. She suggested we drive the old beat up pickup truck to the Central Market at the heart of the city. I quietly contemplated her motives as we made our way to the center of *Limon*.

"I wanted to tell you that our friend Ze'ev Pinsky has extracted more intel from Maziar Safi, the man who attacked you with his son," said Chava. "The banker Mr. Sabo stole money from several head honchos, and Pinsky's target *Vespula* is one of those people. Maziar Safi handled *Vespula's'* money transfers, and now he's on the hook...he is scared shitless, and that's why he's talking. Ze'ev also had the banker's daughter Mimi Sabo tailed. She and her mother left Los Angeles and are now here in Costa Rica, in the capitol. They traveled with the man you know...*Aguilera*. We believe that *Vespula*, Mimi Sabo, and *Aguilera* may all be in contact, perhaps even working together."

"Nothing surprises me...and what of the mother..."

"Senora Sabo? Just a concerned wife, it would seem. Oblivious to the larger picture."

For that reason alone I fought off the urge to bail and cut my losses. She was clean, not dirty like her daughter Mimi and the others…and I had already taken her front money. I looked over and studied Chava's pretty profile carefully.

"And…you chose to tell me these things because…"

"I chose to tell you because my primary duty is to help Pinsky kill *Vespula,* to ensure he never bombs anyone else. Sabo, this crooked banker, he means nothing to us. He is expendable, as is his wife and his daughter. I will help you get Sabo if I can, but it is not primary. Don't get it twisted, as they say."

"If what you say is true, then I am expendable too…"

"Not to me, you're not… Not to Ze'ev either."

"But to your bosses…"

She didn't respond and that said a lot. We didn't speak much more, she just drove. I took in the sights once we parked outside the Central Market area and went on foot. There were local housewives out shopping for food, older men huddling around fruit stands, smoking unfiltered cigarettes, and kids selling cheap souvenirs to conspicuously dressed tourists. Evening was falling and neon signs sparkled eerily upon the timeworn streets. The buildings stood tired, heavy, wanting for upkeep. *Limon* looked older at night. Quite a few nice-looking women stood around too—some not so nice—haunting the bars, tempting foreign men with alluring smiles, hoping for some action…none wasted glances on me, obviously due to Chava's presence.

"This place looks different at night," I said, noting the dilapidated state of most buildings.

"That's part of the charm, I suppose," commented Chava. "There's supposed to be a parade tonight. I thought you might like it, just to break the monotony…"

We didn't have to wait long. Soon, the sound of a Jamaican band filled the tropical air as it made its way down the main boulevard. The tourists and the locals forgot about their usual business and began lining up along the street. The Afro-Latin beat seemed to hypnotize them all, and then the procession of black musicians came into view. A drummer led the way, followed by a horn section and dancers in bright attire. *Limon's* humble version of the *Festival Flora de Diáspora Africana b*egan kicking into high gear. It wasn't much, but it was loud and lively and the curious throngs began singing and clapping along. The small parade advanced frenetically, like an agitated serpent.

I liked the rhythmic cadence and felt somewhat drawn to the black voices erupting above the loud music. Chava seemed less captivated, almost weary. When our eyes met the hardened agent had softened very little.

"You like?" she asked. "This is nothing compared to the capitol," She sounded almost indifferent. "In *San Jose* the celebrations are far more elaborate...I have seen them a few times." All the while her eyes scanned the crowd methodically, like a gazelle marking lions at the water hole.

"A pity you can't really enjoy it, Chava" I said.

"Nor you, to be honest. Unfortunately, downtown *Limon* can be a treacherous place at times, Phillip..." Her frank tone doused the tropical enchantment. The brash band played on, of course, and the lively dancers still swayed, but she stayed leery. It was a good thing, I knew. We weren't exactly newlyweds on a honeymoon.

"Chava, there must be a reason you took us out of the School to talk. What's that reason..."

She turned to look at me. "Smart man...my operation is compromised, Phillip. I am not sure by whom...perhaps that CIA man, Fields, perhaps one of my own. Strange as it may seem, you're a more trusted asset than those I work closest with—and don't doubt for a second you haven't been thoroughly checked out. So listen. Tonight, actually tomorrow morning, we strike this place called 'The Hole.' I am sure Ze'ev Pinsky filled you in on its significance. That's where Sabo is. If

Ze'ev is right, *Vespula* will be there too." I wondered what made them so sure, but I never got a chance to ask.

A woman screamed behind us just then…shrieked …high and piercing… over the blare of the parade trumpets. Chava glanced but dismissed it; it meant nothing in her world. I on the other hand peered over my shoulder, straight down an alley that split two bars, one called *Clavos* and the other called *Mininos. B*oth were stark and neither lacked for danger… I could just tell. But the bars and their patrons did not concern me. Down the alley that split those bars, that's where the trouble was.

A woman in a trampy little dress, if you could even call it that, had just hit the ground screaming…a working girl with a big butt and sturdy legs. I saw her teeth grimace by the red glow of a light bulb blazing above the door she tumbled through. She wore gold heels and one had snapped off like a twig. A big man in a dark suit followed her out the door, lumbering and yelling in hot Spanish and waving an empty whiskey bottle like a cave man with a club. It looked like he wanted to slug her with it but he didn't. He made out to, but instead he stomped her one or two times—good stomps—then bent down and grabbed her hair. Up she rose, light as a half-mannequin, screaming, as he dragged her back towards the bar. She twisted and attempted to break free, but the broken heel tripped her up, and the man slapped her around for trying. Then, with her hair still clenched in his fist, he side-kicked both legs right out from under her. She landed, unceremoniously, flat on her bottom and howled. It wasn't pretty. Some onlookers laughed, but I didn't find it amusing.

Nobody—and I mean nobody—did a damn thing…not one of the parade spectators, not one of the bars' patrons, not even an old municipal cop manning the parade. They all just watched for a while, chuckled or frowned and then turned back to the street show. The only real protester was a little black and tan dog in the alley that kept barking at the man and lunging at his shoes whenever it could. I started to walk over…

"Leave it alone, Phillip. It's not our business. She's nobody, just a whore. Street discipline. Let it go."

I turned and looked back at Chava Cresca.

"I can't let it go…"

Yeah, I knew she was right, but the girl kept shrieking and the big man kept slapping her…and then he hauled off and kicked the tough little dog, too. He caught it good, mid lunge, just under the chest, a real pro-bowl punt. The feisty little champ yelped, sailed up like a football and slammed up against the alley wall with a thud, like a sack of brown sugar. Then it slid down the wall and lay there, out for the count.

That did it for me. Enough was enough, in my book.

I ran down the alley, not really thinking, I guess, and the man looked over with the meanest grimace I had seen in a while. I slowed to a fast walk and right when I got to him, he raised two fingers to his lips and whistled, then swung that empty whisky bottle right at my head.

I instinctively made him miss and penetrated the opening he left with a hard flurry of sledgehammer punches to his chest and head that drove him back, and followed through with an elbow, smack-dab in the middle of his forehead. That last hit, bone to bone, sent him reeling and bowled him over onto his back. I felt and heard every one of those strikes and made them count, rapid-fire and hard. He was too big to take chances on, for sure. The whiskey bottle flew out of his hand as he landed on the ground…it bounced and pinged on the pavement, unbroken, and came to rest right next to the gal in the skimpy dress. The big fellow looked up from the ground, but not at me…just into the faraway *Limon* sky. If he saw any stars they were in his own head. I don't think he knew where he was anymore, but he knew he was through fighting. When his head fell to the side, it was bedtime… out cold.

I had precious little time to assess the damage or tend to the girl. Things happened pretty fast.

"*Cuidado!*" the girl yelled, through the pain and over the drone of the parade, now receding. "*Cuidado!*" she cried again, pointing behind me. "*Sus humbres!*"

The side door of *Mininos* burst open and three more a-holes rushed out, probably summoned by the boss man's whistle, all toting pool cues and 'rearin' to go' from the looks of things. One of them cursed and charged straight at me...a big mistake. Everything I did from that point was pure instinct. Nothing was planned. I dodged his first vicious roundhouse swing and took a stance as he swung again. I dodged again, barely, and caught him with a high, arching classic kick, straight from the hip. My foot cracked his jaw hard and his eyes lit up like spotlights. I landed two more quick punches that flattened his nose and buckled his Adam's apple. He faded silently, then fell back as stiff as a burnt pine. In one quick motion I grabbed the pool cue from his limp hands and whirled, barely in time to block an overhead tomahawk swing from another man. I lunged forward with the butt of the cue and brutally jabbed that guy's solar plexus, then twisted to deflect a swing from number three.

To be frank, I like nothing better than a good stick fight...I'm like a shark in warm waters...and it didn't take long for them to figure out that they had their hands full. But I had my hands full too, because two more rushed from the bar, one armed with a bottle and the other with what I thought was a baseball bat. The guy with the bottle got it first. I crowned him king of the night—top of his skull—and he toppled over with his eyes still open. I only caught a glimpse of the bat, which turned out to be a rounded two-by-four, but fended off the swing that brought it to me. My pool cue shattered, but probably saved half my rib cage. I grabbed the swinger's forearm, yanked him to me and nailed his face with my opposite elbow. He threw his free arm around me and drove me hard against the bar's brick wall. He had me pinned, but a wild swing from one of the pool cues cracked him instead of me, and I broke free—with the two-by-four now in my possession. There were two left with pool sticks, and one man disarmed and hot, and he stooped down and grabbed the butt-end handle of the shattered pool cue. It was three on one now, but I had the big equalizer in hand and by that time I was *pissed off!*

"Vamos!" I roared. *"Soy listo!"*

And come they did, like three swinging tornadoes. For every blow that came my way, I countered with blocks, parries and counterstrikes that put a bad-ass hurting on each one of them. If I got hit, I never felt it. They were getting hammered, but they fought and didn't quit; I'll give them that much. One more went down hard and the last two suddenly wised up. They tried to flank me on either side, rushing at angles. I retreated against the alley wall, but only briefly. I had that big-ass stick, mind you, and after a few more counter-cracks and one telling jab to somebody's family jewels, I regained the initiative. They rushed once more and I knew I had to finish them before my luck ran out. Everything suddenly speeded up then. I jab-stepped, but lost my footing on a chunk of broken pool cue, and hit the deck.

I thought I was a goner.

One moved in with a shout, but just before he struck, that little black and tan dog came out of nowhere and ripped into his calf. He hollered and convulsed, and swung at the dog instead. I seized the moment and struck with fury, crushing a shin and shattering his kneecap, then desperately rolled away and onto my feet as he shrieked in pain. The last man rushed me and swung the heavy end of his pool stick so hard it whistled and rattled the bones of my arms when I blocked it. Another swing whizzed by just inches from my face, and all the while that little dog kept dodging in and out, nipping at the man's shins and growling like a little badger, ferocious and fearless.

Then I heard sirens and saw Chava running toward us with her Jericho 941. I knew she would do something but I didn't know what, so I took a big chance and feigned a swing at that last adversary, and then put everything I had into a backward roundhouse kick, chin high. The risk paid off, because the roundhouse kick sent him sailing across the alley like he'd been hit with a Joe Frazier uppercut…it was devastating…the guy actually sailed off his feet and stumbled backwards before losing it and slamming the back of his head into the wall, if you can believe that. But I did pay a price. I felt a thunderbolt whip across my back as a pool cue landed. The big man in the suit had risen to strike again.

I tumbled forward to the pavement with a grunt. The rounded two-by-four stick flew from my grasp. I rolled, more to avoid another strike than from the actual back blow itself. Still, I was down. Defenseless. I knew I was in trouble. The big suited man moved in, limping and grimacing with pain and hatred. He swung the pool stick down hard and heavy, going for my head. Somehow, I made him miss.

He raised it high again but suddenly Chava Cresca, shouting *"Kee-yahh!"* flew into him with both feet first, full-force, catapulting her entire mass into his midsection, and knocking him completely off his feet. His body seemed to fly in all directions at once…his pool cue bounced and spun like a drumstick before finally resting on the pavement. The man crash-landed right beside the gal with the broken shoe heel. He tried to rise, but before he could, the girl grabbed the whiskey bottle beside her and slammed it down on the top of his head…and that time, it *did* break, shattering into pieces. It was over.

All three of us, Chava, the girl and I, were on the ground too. Slowly, we rose together, trying to get our legs back. The little black and tan dog rushed the man in the three piece suit and sank his teeth into the man's shoe, snarling and tugging at the laces with little effect. The battle had ended, but he still remembered who had kicked him.

The sight of it made me laugh a little.

"Phillip…you are crazy!" cried Chava. I wasn't sure if she was pissed off or amazed, or maybe a combination of both. "You're unpredictable, incorrigible…I don't really know *what* you are but… damn…you sure know how to fight." She looked over at the girl with the broken heel, who had never let go of the broken neck of the whiskey bottle. "We don't even know her…and everybody's looking… we better go…*now*. *I*'ll handle the police, but I'm not happy about this at all!"

I nodded. "I'm not your typical spectator, Chava. I don't turn my back on people. Maybe that disqualifies me for *Mossad* or the CIA, but…just tell me this, if it was your sister…or your mother, would you have done the same?"

"Let's just go, Phillip." Chava looked at the working girl one more time. Finally she asked in Spanish, "Where will you go?" The girl looked toward the bar, then back at Chava, and shrugged. She had nobody. "Fine then…go with him," she said, pointing at me. "He likes to save everybody. Maybe he'll find a place for you, too." She glared at me one last time, but I didn't get that she was all that mad. She turned away and stalked off to charm the now-arriving police.

"And the dog comes too," I said, to the girl.

"He no mine," she said. "He nobody *perro.*"

"Go grab 'im then, quick," I said, motioning with a hand. I tapped my chest. "He's mine now. Hurry!"

CHAPTER 14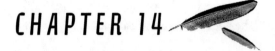

The girl's name was *Anjela*. She didn't seem too concerned about the broken heel on her gold shoe. Her eyes were honey-brown, arresting, and set off by orange highlights in her hair that looked like she aimed for blond streaks but somehow came up short. She also possessed a quality seen in a lot of women doing her type of work...alluring sexuality.

She had no place to go; she made that clear. She couldn't go back to the *Clavos* bar. The fight had burned her bridges...those boys wouldn't take kindly to having their asses kicked by an Americano. She said they would probably kill her, or maybe cut up her face to set an example. She tried to talk in broken English, apparently to accommodate me.

She sat in the middle, between myself and Chava, and kept her hands neatly folded on her lap. For some reason she didn't seem to fit my idea of a prostitute. She seemed like a nice girl gone bad.

"What's its name?" I finally asked—the little dog seemed to have found its comfort zone in my lap.

"Clavos...I teenk," said the girl, staring in my eyes. "Dat what da man say."

"What man?"

She struggled to answer and Chava plugged her with a series of rapid–fire questions in Spanish. She rattled off her answers just as fast.

"She says some Anglo left it behind. He spoke English, but not

American. Maybe a Brit," suggested Chava. "Steady customer for a while. He just disappeared one day. The dog stayed behind."

"What, he named it after some bar?" I asked. It seemed plausible. "Clavos," I said. "Clavos!" The dog stared straight ahead taking no note of my voice. "Not his name..."

Chava shook her head. "Don't think so. That's just what she calls it. The Brit told her its name in Spanish is Clavos...same as the bar. Coincidence I bet."

"Well what does Clavos mean in English," I asked, scratching the dog's floppy black ears.

"Hmm, I don't know really. It doesn't translate well...old decorative nails? Maybe his name is Nails, or Tacky or Rusty, who knows? It didn't react when you called it Clavos just now, did it... but it does seem to like you. It's cute I guess, if you like little dogs."

"I like little tough ones. You don't like dogs, Chava?"

"Not my thing. Cats either. Not a pet person. I had a chameleon once. It got away. Didn't bother looking for it."

"Nice. Ask her where's she from."

"Already did. *San Jose*...the capital. Said she can't go back there either. She's not wanted for arrest, though. Doesn't want to say why. Bet it's her family. You'll never guess exactly where she's from... *Los Guido.*"

"The little shanty town? Come on, you're shitting me..."

"Nope," said Chava. "Says she grew up there. Knows the place like the back of her hand."

I looked her over again. I had my doubts. Who could blame me after all I'd been through? "Seems like quite a coincidence...almost too convenient."

Chava shrugged. "Not really. These whore types move from city to city sometimes. Wear out the welcome, move on. Doesn't look to be anything more than what she is. Pretty girl."

"Can't argue." I turned to the girl. "So you're from *San Jose*?" She understood and nodded. *"Y tu nombre..."*

"Anjela. Mi nombre es Anjela."

"Su nombre completo?"

"Angela Solis Bravo," she mumbled, looking over at Chava. I got the distinct feeling she didn't trust me. I tapped her shoulder and stared into her face again. She didn't like that either...she even looked a little fearful. After seeing me go hard in that brawl, I got that. But I meant her no harm, so I tried to let my tone of voice show it.

"Bravo?" It seemed too coincidental to believe. "You got family here...in *Limon*?"

"My family from *San Jose*. All of dem. From *Los Guido* like I say. I no lie to you. You da big boss now? You no boss of me." Talk about attitude; she had plenty to spare.

"Let me talk to her," said Chava. "She doesn't trust you. I can see that..." Chava did her thing again, and when she finished she said, "She's nineteen, Phillip. Her family made her leave *San Jose* once she started working. They're Catholic and poor...big family. She brought shame on them by tricking, so she came here to *Limon* with her brother about a year ago. Her father is a mechanic who works for some church. Her mother cleans house for the same people. She has three brothers and four sisters...she actually had four brothers but one is dead, the one who came with her to *Limon*. She says he got shot by the police half a year ago...strange circumstances. Now she's alone." Chava reached over and touched the girl's leg. It was the first sign of compassion I had seen her display. "I believe her, Phillip... anything else?"

Yeah, just one more thing. What was his name? The brother..."

"Ricardo." The girl said, answering the question herself. *"Él está muerto...la policia. Ellos le derribó."*

"She says they shot him in cold blood."

"I got it." I nodded, with a sinking feeling in my stomach. "Ricardo Bravo...as in Rico Bravo?"

The girl reacted immediately and stared at me with a look of absolute fear. *"Es usted la policía?"*

"No," I said. *Absolutamente No.*"

"What's going on here?" asked Chava.

"I'll explain it all later," I said, still taking it in. "It'll be an interesting bedtime story. That's for sure."

CHAPTER 15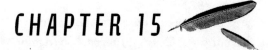

Once back inside in my room, I revisited the dossiers of *Aguilera* and *Vespula*, the ones supplied to me by Temple. The good doctor's facts proved fascinating even through a second reading. I had little reason to doubt their accuracy... the data came from multiple intelligence sources, including the CIA and British Intelligence.

Vespula was a hot target indeed, as Ze'ev had stated. Born in Tehran but raised and educated in England, his file disclosed prior employment with Britain's MI6 as a translator, a freelance assassin, and a top-level courier. He had once been reliable, had played the British spy game exceedingly well and had gained significant knowledge of Western tracking techniques along the way. Those factors in themselves made him a formidable adversary. But somewhere along the line *Vespula* had switched allegiance to the Arab terrorist groups. He had also undergone extensive plastic surgery in Iran... no one knew what he looked like anymore, not even Ze'ev Pinsky. The guy was good, very good.

Aguilera's file was more scant. On paper he looked clean as a whistle, with contacts in American law enforcement and upstanding relatives living in the U.S. The CIA's only concern was how easily large quantities of cocaine moved through Costa Rica on his watch. Still, he was not considered a threat to vital interests. He had even proved useful to the CIA despite his reputation for graft and greed...just another tool who posed little threat beyond his own little drug turf. That didn't stop me from holding a distinct personal grudge. I don't like little tin gods who kill with impunity, wherever they rule.

At midnight, Chava Cresca came knocking.

"*Anjela* is sleeping. I gave her a room and a change of clothes. She'll probably be gone in the morning." Chava shrugged. "So frigging young…"

"Yeah," I said quietly. "You know what? If I hadn't met her brother my last time through, he might still be alive. I wasn't about to tell *her* that…but it's a small damn world."

"Are you going to tell me about it?"

"About what happened? Sure. I said I would. You'll be the first person I've told and quite probably the last…" Chava was so good to look at, just standing there. "Nice tank top and field shorts there Chava, very mod, but not exactly practical you know. No weapon?"

"Oh, I'm armed…as always Phillip. After you tell me that bedtime story like you promised, I'll let you look for it." She sat on my bed next to the little black dog with such relaxed familiarity that I almost forgot she could kill me a half-dozen ways without ever hoisting a pistol. The dog, which had been twitching in sleep for some time looked up at her casually, then lowered its head and calmly resumed its rest.

"So…what happened?"

"Well, for starters, have you ever heard the term, "gunwalking?"

"No.."

"It's an American term. Gunwalking is when agents, say Alcohol, Tobacco and Firearms agents, know that guns are being purchased illegally by some drug cartel underling, but do nothing. They let the guy go, hoping the guns will lead him to the higher-ups. They do it all the time with narcotics or sensitive documents. The danger with guns is that they can get lost in the shuffle. Then they're just out there, being used to kill people…the wrong people. Get it?"

"Yeah. It's a gamble…an organizational gamble."

"Right. Last year some guys in the Department of Justice okayed the gunwalking plan for ATF in Arizona, by the U.S. border with

Mexico. It was called Operation Fast and Furious and it was orchestrated out of Phoenix. Hundreds of military weapons were purchased
by *Los Zetas*, the most violent drug cartel in Mexico, and ATF knew
about it and let it happen.

"*Los Zetas*?"

"Drug cartel…killers…the heads in a duffel bag sort."

"Mmm… my kind of guys," said Chava. "I love plugging them."

"Yeah, right," I retorted. "It all blew up in their faces a year later
when three Border Patrol agents and two *Los Zetas* drug smugglers
died in a shootout at the border. The cops found two AK-47 assault
rifles, in the hands of the dead smugglers. They were both traced
back to Operation Fast and Furious. No drugs or money at the scene,
though."

"Okay…sounds like just another ambush by a rival cartel. But
what does that have to do with you, and Costa Rica, and that kid Rico
Bravo."

"Well come to find out, lo and behold, the Department of Justice
denied all involvement. Leaders at the ATF backpedaled too, and said
the whole operation was run by a bunch of rogue agents…total denial.
Standard practice probably. But one of the ATF agents had secretly
recorded meetings in the planning stages of the operation. That agent's
name was Voshe. Those recordings prove that leaders at the highest
level of DOJ were involved. That in turn jeopardized the reputation
of the White House, first term president and all. The Senate Judiciary
Committee started investigating, and suddenly the ATF agent with all
the recordings disappeared."

"Voshe?"

"Correct. Guess where he ran off to?

"Costa Rica?"

"Precisely…into the wind, just like that."

"And that's where you come in…"

"Yeah. Believe it or not, a ranking member of the Senate Judiciary
Committee secretly hired me to find the guy and convince him to

participate in the investigation. Or maybe they just wanted him back in the United States so they could expedite their damage control…no telling."

"In exchange for what…criminal immunity?"

"That perhaps, or maybe just his normal life back again. All that really mattered is that somebody wanted him back and they were willing to pay me top dollar to make it happen. I found him too…."

CHAPTER 16

My first knowledge of Fast and Furious came from a Congressional page named Al Grissom. Grissom worked for John Grant, a senator who sat on the Senate Judiciary Committee. Grissom told me his boss Grant was trying to locate an ex-ATF agent, the guy named Voshe. Voshe had retired when all the F&F crap hit the fan...and incidentally, he was also friends with one of the border patrol guys who got pasted to the ground. Voshe quit ATF without notice, cashed in his vacation and other time off and left the U.S. for parts unknown.

My job was to find Voshe, get him back to Arizona and ensure he met with Senator John Grant. I wasn't exactly sure about Grant's political motives, but he offered up my standard fee with a big bonus proviso for total confidentiality...not exactly a problem on my end.

My secretary Charity quickly located Voshe's older brothers and sisters in New Mexico, as well as two cousins living in Utah. I found it strange that no one ever bothered questioning them before. Voshe's siblings claimed he bolted after he got death threats from Mexican drug lords and angry co-workers. Nobody explained the reason to my satisfaction... and if they knew his location, they weren't spilling any beans to me.

I finally hit pay dirt when I met Voshe's seventy-nine year old widowed mother. Her husband had died ten years prior; he was a decorated Korean War vet and a cabinet maker. She was old and lonely and maybe that's why she drank and talked so much. She spent the entire time trying to convince me what a great guy Voshe was.

Thing was, her big house in Baldwin Hills looked totally renovated, top to bottom, and I immediately wondered who paid for it all. She said it was her son's second home. That set off alarm bells in my head. Unless Voshe was working serious overtime, there was no way he could afford that place, especially since according to Charity he had been divorced three times. But there his mother was, living on a scenic hill in California, peering down on poor neighbors she had lived with for most of her life— until six months prior. She even had an in-home registered nurse at her beck and call.

I soothed and charmed her well. Eventually, Mrs. Voshe told me her little angel had run off to Costa Rica with a Mexican girlfriend. She wasn't supposed to tell anybody. She only told me, she said, because she knew I was a good man, like her son.

According to her, he lived by the beach...*how nice.*

Needless to say, I was on the next plane to *San Jose*, Costa Rica. *Lineas Aereas Costarricenses* —LACSA— the national airline of Costa Rica, had a non-stop red-eye out of LAX that flew straight to the capital...I managed to pull some strings. First Class too, the only seat available on such short notice, so it was costly. But seven hours after take-off, I was in Costa Rica.

———

I first met young Rico Bravo at the *San Juantamaria* Airport in the capital . He was working a taxi just outside baggage claim. He offered to take my bags with a flourish of insincere courtesy and then immediately pegged me as an African American tourist looking for sex. First he offered to drive me to a corner he said had 'hot connections', and 'real good pieces of tail.' When I chuckled at his misconception and told him I was there strictly on business, he immediately switched gears. He declared himself the best English speaking business guide in *San Jose*. In fact, he was pretty insistent about it.

Once inside the kid's musky-smelling taxi, the first thing I noticed was his elaborate tattoos…all in vivid color and exceptionally detailed, up and down his arms and extending up past his collar. I assumed his hair covered some on his head, too. But again, the quality appeared outstanding. Somebody clearly knew what they were doing. Then I noticed how fast he talked English, despite a noticeably thick accent.

"Where to?"

I already knew where to find Voshe. He had purchased beachfront property with cash. All land acquisition by foreigners is carefully monitored by the Ministry of the Interior and the Costa Rican courts— and Charity Fields is the best; need I say more?

"Just drive, *amigo*. I want to get a feel for the place first. After that I'll need a decent hotel. I already booked one but maybe you know something I don't? For now, show me the city…your city, *mi hombre*." I wanted to milk Rico Bravo for any helpful information I could.

When I asked him about his tattoos , he said he inked most himself.

"You'd have to be good with both hands, buddy…"

"Yeah amigo, I am. I'm not just a good tattoo artist, I'm the best in Coast Rica…*I* think so. It's how I got by in the jails. I got paid to do it, real money, sometimes even by guards. If a guy inside didn't have no money I did it for food or maybe some of his stuff. I am self-trained. I do it for whatever I need. I've done a lot of tattoos, *jefe*. Women, men, even young pigs."

"Pigs?"

"Yes for farmers, or sometimes just for practice. That's how I got so good. I will do anything for anybody. You would not believe all the different body parts I've done. This one guy had me do a two-headed blue dragon on his--"

"I get the picture, kid. Not pretty. Did you ever tattoo somebody in exchange for narcotics? Just curious…"

"What makes you think that?" he asked.

"Just a guess…" I said. "Saw some tracks on your left arm, through the nice tats. I guess I notice things like that, but don't take it personal. Everybody's got issues."

"You got tattoos, *jefe?*" He ignored my observations, which I found amusing.

"Yeah," I said, with a chuckle. "One on each shoulder…a lion and a gorilla."

"Good work?"

"Not too shabby. By the way, where did you learn to talk English so well?"

"I lived for a while in The States."

"Really?"

"Yes. I ran away to America when I was fifteen years old. I got deported three or four times, every time for dope…heroin. Yes, you called it right, *jefe*. I couldn't stop using. But the last time I got deported, they sent me to Mexico, *jefe*. They didn't believe me when I said I was from Costa Rica! They got me mixed up with another Mexican Mafia *ese* named Rico Bravo. I kept telling them that my name is *Ricardo* Bravo, but they wouldn't listen. They dumped me off in *Tijuana*. T.J. sucks, *jefe*. I started doing tattoos just for food money. After that, I came back home for good. I'm all cleaned up now, though. No more *drogas*. Now I'm a born again Christian."

"Is that so," I asked, with jaded reservations. It sounded like he tossed that last bit out like a peanut to a pigeon, but I carried on. "So where did you find Jesus? In the American jail or while inking tattoos for tacos in Mexico?"

He caught my humor and laughed.

"No *Americano*, I'm not shitting you. I have changed. I got my own place in *Limon* now. Got a little sister living here with me and I've got to take care of her. She works too."

"Yeah, doing what?"

"Just odd jobs. We take care of each other."

"Good to hear all that. Family's gotta take care of family. Plus, I wouldn't hire you if I knew you were still on that crap.

"Oh no way, *jefe*, those days are behind me now. I got a lot to be clean for. My little sister, she's real nice to tourists who come to town. They all like her. If you want…I'll introduce you to her. She's young, *jefe*. You know…*tight*…and we need the money.

He was crude, but I liked his spirit of entrepreneurship. He just kept begging for my business and wouldn't take no for an answer. It became a classic case of "all right-already"… I was new to Costa Rica and the job was just a low-key 'locate and contact' so I decided to take him on.

"I don't want your little sister. But if you want money….there's a little beach town on the western coast. It's a drive, though. Take me there. I'll pay you three hundred American, *if* you get me there by noon. That's a lot more than your sister can make in a day, no matter how nice she is. Three hundred American for half a day's work …you understand *that* English?

"*Chido, mi hombre*! I just scored big-time, brotha!"

"I'll see Rico…Remember though…by noon."

You will see! What town again, *jefe*?

"I didn't say yet, Rico…"

CHAPTER 17

The kid drove me to *Jaco* and I directed him to Voshe's place. It was just a nice bungalow really, very small with a big front yard and a short stroll to the sandy beach. It sat away from all the big condos and the fancy haciendas…a nice place to escape to. I thought it would be the easiest money I ever made. That's how lax I felt about the whole thing… silly me. I gave Rico Bravo half his money and told him to get himself a lunch and come back in twenty minutes. I was toting a shoulder bag with a wordy letter from Senator Gradwell and other papers promising Voshe immunity, so long as he cooperated and played no role in the Border Patrol killings.

Two black Chevy vans and a bronze Pontiac Aztec—maybe the ugliest SUV I've ever seen—were parked in the graveled driveway. I thought nothing of the vans just then, but maybe I should have…

I walked up to the big front door and knocked, not too hard, and rang the doorbell for good measure. I heard movement on the other side of the door. A female began chattering softly, but no one answered, so I knocked again harder and waited. Still no answer…

"Mr. Voshe," I said loudly, "If you're home please come to the door. I have important news for you." Finally the door opened. A young Latina in tight jeans and a puffy blue blouse filled the threshold.

"Who the fugg are you?" she asked coldly. She had dyed her hair orange, slapped on foundation as thick as a death mask, and painted her eyelids in a 'queen of the Nile' style worn by pretentious young *chicas* craving exoticism. It didn't work out well; in fact it bombed, but at least I'll never forget the look.

"Jarred Singleton." It was my standard cover. Every document I had bore it out. "I need to speak to Mr. Voshe…"

"What's this about, mister? We ain't buyin' nothin."

"Not at liberty to say…on behalf of the United States Government." She was obviously American, so I didn't say anything more. She looked over her shoulder, then back at me.

"You have no authority here, asshole," she said. She was agitated and her pupils were dilated…obviously high on something or other.

"True…I'm not law enforcement. But I am authorized to contact the local Judicial Police here in *Jaco* if I find it necessary to do so." Sure I was bluffing, but how would she know that? "It would so much easier if I could just talk to Voshe. Is he at home or not?"

She wavered, then glanced back again. "No."

"Fine," I said, and pulled my cell phone from its holster. I started dialing random numbers.

"Wait. That's not necessary," she said. "I'm sorry, mister, we had some trouble here. I didn't know you were government. If you wait, I'll get Voshe…"

"That's fine," I said. "But my time is limited…"

"Of course…" She closed the door gently in my face…I waited. After a while, the doorknob turned slowly and the door swung open again.

"Mr. Voshe will see you now. Please enter."

I took a step forward and peered ahead as I prepared to enter. A huge landscape of a seaside Tuscan village dominated the wall behind her. It was glass-covered, and in its reflection I saw myself and the back of her head. She turned to follow my gaze, and as she did so, I saw a figure standing behind the opened door. It was a man, and he held a *machete* in both hands, like a samurai before a ceremonial beheading. A section of blade glimmered in the sunlight. She saw what I could see—her eyes reacted—and she opened her mouth to speak, but before any utterance I slammed my shoulder into the door with all my might, pinning the man with a jarring blow.

The door recoiled and I shoulder-slammed it again. The chunky girl screamed an alarm and ran toward the back of the house. I swung the door open quickly, stepped around it and swung. My fist slammed into the side of his head, and I kept right on punching as he raised the machete with his left hand. The blade reached its apex and I pinned his wrist, then grabbed his hair and smashed his head into the wall. The cheap plaster caved in, but I kept bashing his skull until he crumpled. The machete blade clanked loudly onto the tiled floor. I heard multiple footsteps and knew more trouble was coming...

I picked up the machete in time to see another man rush me with a machete of his own. He was short and squat and swung his blade with sweeping cuts, always advancing. I tried maneuvering but he knew how to cut me off while never leaving himself exposed. I blocked his swings defensively, but they came fast and hard and I found myself backing away until was I pressed to the wall with nowhere to go. I think I might have died right then if a third man had not rushed into the room, machete-armed, and tried to get a lick in while I fended off my primary attacker. I flinched downward, and just that little movement caused the second man's blade to whistle over my head so closely it would have given me a brush-cut if I had any hair. The heart of that blade's edge dug into the wall and got stuck there, and I used the sharp side of my weapon to drive into the second attacker, which pushed him into the first man's downward stroke. The blow severed his left shoulder down to the bones. He howled, and I swung my weapon past his opposite shoulder just as my primary raised his hands defensively to stop the coming blow. Human flesh does not stop a machete blade, and my attacker learned that personally when his four right fingers and a small portion of his thumb landed on the tile floor. As he screamed, I planted the bottom of my foot squarely into his gaping chin, and just as he hit the floor, I was driving my opposite foot into the lateral knee of his woeful comrade...

I never saw the hit that knocked me out, but when I came to, I found myself hogtied in Voshe's back yard with *Aguilera* standing over me, sending out some very unpleasant vibes. I barely made out his face because the sun glared in my eyes, but I'll never forget the sight of him clutching my documents in one hand and a big, bloody *Condor* machete in the other. He was agitated, to say the least. He stared me down, lifted the long blade high over his head with a hiss and swung it down with all his might... I yelled like a slaughterhouse pig and just about shit my pants. The *Condor* sliced the soft earth inches from my head, and I gasped, counting myself lucky to be alive.

A chorus of laughter from across Voshe's grassy back lawn filled the air and I looked toward the wicked cackles. Four or five men huddled in a group around a big blue tarp. One of them smiled at me and pointed a finger toward the ground. That's when I saw the carnage.

Voshe, or what remained of him, lay strewn on the plastic blue tarp, chopped up in chunky pieces. It was a bloody mess. They had literally slaughtered him like a farm animal. One leg and two arms still remained, and a good portion of his torso lay off to the side. The lady with the thick eye liner—the one who had answered the door--held Voshe's head in her right fist. It dangled thigh-high from his stringy wet hair, shifting at her side as she eyed the scene dispassionately...calmly... like a woman clutching a handbag at a bus stop.

What a way to go...

Voshe's mouth, strangely slack, hung wide open. His blood-stained tongue stuck out too, like a 'take-a-number' meat market pull tab. I knew right then that *my* number had been called— not a pleasant sensation, believe me.

"You see this fat *calabazo*, tough guy?" asked the leering lady as the head hung at her hip. "That's right, its pumpkin season...and guess what? You're next. I'm gonna chop you up, just like I did this fool...boil you right down, too! That's how we *Ticas* roll here in Costa Rica." She hoisted Voshe's head a little higher for emphasis, and then plopped it casually into a liquid-filled barrel standing beside her. I heard a gentle splash and a fizzling hiss, and more soft laughter from the butchers all around her.

Aguilera nudged my shoulder with his foot. "We don't tolerate *Americanos* butting into our affairs, Mr. Singleton…making trouble….I don't like it…and you see how I deal with troublesome *Americanos*. Except now you come with these papers from the American government…a senator in fact. If you don't want to end up like that *Anglo,* start talking *amigo.*"

CHAPTER 18

Chava blinked and stared at me, and I wasn't sure what she was thinking. "How did you get out of that one alive?" Chava asked. "You told him everything…"

"Of course. I wasn't exactly keeping state secrets, and he could read English. Naturally he rifled through the documents, started asking questions. He didn't seem too happy that the U.S. government wanted Voshe, and once he verified I was sent by a United States senator, he changed his murderous attitude rather quickly. I'm still not sure why he didn't kill me. I guess he didn't want the negative attention. I know now that he was coming up on a big promotion, the one he just got to head up drug enforcement in Costa Rica."

"Wow. I guess that promotion was a license to start printing money, huh?"

I chuckled. "For a slime like him, yeah. He had a lot at stake just then…that figured in, I bet. So…after I spilled my beans on the table, he called somebody—stateside, I think—and they talked. Once he got the lowdown, he didn't let the crazy chick cut my damn head off. Maybe he didn't want the hassle. I didn't ask… seemed like a good strategy.

"Yeah, I bet…and *Anjela's* brother?"

"Rico? He returned, just as they were dragging me to one of the black vans out front. He was eating something, and when he saw us he took off like a bat out of hell. Passed up his full fare," I added, partly in jest. "*Aguilera* said something and waved his hand and two of his crew took off after him. That was the last time I saw him alive..."

"And what about Panama..."

"Well, they shoved me into a van and off we drove, south into Panama. No check at the border either, just straight through. They had important business there. They interrogated me the whole time, asked the same questions over and over, and they made threats, but by then I knew they weren't going to kill me."

"No?"

I shrugged. "At least not with a machete... as to why I'm still alive...dumb luck perhaps...but when your head is on the chopping block, who questions the pardon?"

Chava nodded. "Have you ever considered that *Aguilera* was behind Mimi Sabo approaching you?"

"Of course, from the moment I saw him cruising through Santa Monica. I'm not quite that dim-witted. But either way, I want to get that banker out. It's not even about the money anymore, Chava..."

"I know. *Aguilera's* involved. He hurt you and this is a chance for payback. You don't like to lose. It's a man thing."

"It's a Specialist thing. I'd love to get a fair crack at that guy, believe me. And now it's your turn. Tell me what you know."

"Pretty much what you know...*Aguilera's* dirty. He's helping the Columbians move dope on into Mexico. You might be interested to know that one of the Mexican smugglers that got killed in that ATF shootout was a nephew of a *Zetas* big shot who lives in *Limon*. I remember it made the Tico Times. I think Voshe was selling military grade weapons to the *Zetas*. I think he and his border patrol buddies ambushed the nephew for drugs or money, maybe both."

"Makes sense," I said. "It went bad, or maybe it went perfect and then Voshe turned on his friends to get everything. *Aguilera's* move on Voshe was payback. I walked into the middle of that."

"Yes," she said. "He probably didn't kill you for the very reason you say, to keep the Americans out of his business. It stands to reason…he is the top drug cop in Costa Rica now, isn't he?"

"And this *Vespula?* What's the connection?"

"Only one thing comes to mind. All that money your banker Sabo took. Some of it was *Vespula's*, sure. But some of it was cartel money too, and if *Aguilera* is working for the cartels…"

"And of course he is, Chava…"

"Then he's probably under orders to get it back…or maybe he sees a chance to get it all, because the bottom line is that if somebody nabbed Sabo and they haven't killed him already, it's only because he's no good to them dead. Sabo's got to know if he allows anyone access to that money he'll end up like Voshe…"

"And Sabo's wife had to know that if she paid a huge ransom she'd never see him alive again anyway. So she hired me."

"Frankly, Phillip, I think you're working on the cheap, all things considered."

"Yeah," I said. "I get a feeling now that Sabo won't come out of this alive."

"We might not either."

"I plan to." And I meant it. "What kind of weapons does Ze'ev got in that armory. I'm very interested to know that."

"Let's go. You'll see what we've got. I've been trying to contact my people. I wanted us to all meet and brief first, but I can't reach anybody. It's strange, but I can show you the place. We'll need that gear. Things could get hot and heavy in *San Jose*. I hope you're ready for anything."

I nodded, and then looked over at my dog as he rustled in his sleep. "'*Clavos*'…you said his name meant 'nails,' right?"

"Yeah…"

"How about… 'Spike'? The dog snapped his head up and stared at me, and cocked his head in curious recognition. The tail wagged too, so I said the name again… "Hey, Spike." Suddenly, the little guy sprung to his feet, alert and happy. We were both surprised.

"Spike!" said Chava, and he snapped his head in her direction as well. "That's his name...it must be, Phillip. Well, well...You're damn good."

"I try."

CHAPTER 19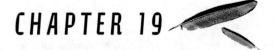

The armory was in the lower part of the building. You could enter from the inside by a security door, and from the outside by a roll-up gate facing an alley running along the back of the building. The whole time we approached, Chava kept trying to contact her operatives ...and I could tell she couldn't. She didn't say anything, but I knew something wasn't quite right. I had a bad feeling when we got there.

My gut feeling was right.

Chava punched in a key code and pushed open the secure door... and there stood CIA Agent Fields, waiting for us with a gun in his hand.

"Welcome, Chava. I've been expecting you. Don't bother trying to signal for help," said Fields testily, waving us in with a small flick of his gun barrel. "Come on in, don't be rude. Shut the door behind you. I took the liberty of...hmm, how should I say it...of *deactivating* your fellow *Mossad* agents while you and your new boyfriend cavorted about town."

"Where are they, you slick bastard?" said Chava. She sounded infuriated, but she never moved her hands from her sides. Fields had us dead to rights and she knew it.

"They're all sitting in your little IT room, my dear, stiff as stones... data flows in, but no more breakdown, no outflow. Now move on in here, you two...carefully." We complied...we knew he would not hesitate to kill us both in an instant. He eyed me like I had punked him for his lunch money when we were kids, and might punk him for his gun if I could. "Don't think you're quicker than my trigger finger, Kung Fu man. I'm actually hoping you'll test me. Both of you sit down on the floor... keep your hands where I can see them."

"So it's been you the whole time, huh Fields?" Chava was remarkably poised for a woman who Fields had little reason to spare. "We've known about the leaks to Hezbollah for some time, but I'm still curious. They started before you ever got here. Care to fill me in?" Despite her training she instinctively looked to the side, her gaze shifting to an old-style 'break the glass' fire alarm on the wall.

"That all-call's been deactivated too, I'm afraid," said Fields. "Wouldn't want every *Mossad* Agent in Central America to know that their little safe house needs help, would we? Yes, Chava, I'm fully informed of your entire procedures. As to how much informed...well, I suppose you could ask one of your greener agents in the IT room—a foolish and rather greedy one, but his lips are sealed forever now, along with everyone else's..."

"I can't believe you'd work for Hezbollah or the likes of *Vespula*," said Chava.

"I don't," said Fields. "I work for myself. I don't give a rat's ass if your people and their people blow each other to smithereens. Israel, Iran, Syria, it's really all the same cesspool. Armageddon, World War Three, one hot quick exchange back to the Stone Age. That's what it's all heading for, right? Me? I'm in it for *me*. I'm not a patsy like *Daniel-san* over there." He pointed at me, gazing with utter contempt. "Isn't that right, Mr. Specialist...wax on, wax off, do whatever that fool Ze'ev Pinsky tells you to do. Not me. I finally wised up. I stopped listening to the false religion of the higher-ups...the same bastards who washed out my career because I refused to play along."

"You mean those rapes in Algiers? You didn't have to clam up. All you had to do was tell the truth," I said.

"Wrong. I couldn't. I couldn't talk about the so-called rapes by my superior in Algiers. I'm the one who filmed them..."

"You filmed them?" Judging by his face, I did a bad job of hiding my scorn.

"Yes—and no, they were not secretly taped. That's what you think? No. I'm not a sick perv. I participated. I helped conduct a CIA-approved interrogation."

"Is that what you call raping women," asked Chava. "An interrogation?"

"That's what it was! They were spies, friends of terrorists! We took the fall for doing our jobs! For doing exactly what they told us to do. They thanked me by sending me here with the likes of you. You're quite the arrogant one, Chava, aren't you? Is there anything you would not do in defense of your own country? Probably not. Me either, at one time. Except that America is quick to sell you out when it all flips bad. That's what they did to me. Now it's all even. *Vespula* is in *San Jose* now to pick up Sabo, and when he does, believe me, he'll get his money back, and I'll get my cut for wiping you all out, like I did your friends upstairs. They're all dead with holes in their heads. I'm a good shot up close."

He kept waving the business end of his gun at us, so we sat and listened. I understood things a little better. Costa Rica was a chessboard where Hezbollah and the *Mossad* played out their little strategies on neutral ground, where the innocents and the victims were not their own citizens...*oh my, how bloody- well convenient!* Fields just spotted an opportunity and sold out for a pocketful of silver.

I wondered how much of his story was true, and how much was just lies he filled his own head with. All the while I kept looking at the stockpile of guns and explosives stacked floor to ceiling. They were useless to me, so long as Fields had the upper hand.

"Fields, listen," I said finally. He turned his head with the fluid coldness of a cobra on point. I felt like he shot me between the eyes, his frosty gaze doing the work. "*Vespula* has killed dozens, and if you help him he'll kill hundreds more, maybe thousands. You could help us take this guy down and save countless lives. Is that really what you stand for…sick, merciless bombings, lifetimes of pain…all for money?" It sounded banal, but it was all I had.

Fields did not even blink. "Yeah, that's exactly what I stand for. Don't got a problem with that…I'm CIA, remember? I leave guilt to grasshoppers like you. So, on to my business…both of you… lie down on the floor, *now*…and Chava, I swear to God if you so much as twitch wrong I'll kill you first, then lover-boy. Don't try me."

He was going to kill us both no matter what; I figured that. Neither one of us wanted to go out like that.

"Lay down!" He had a charm that was hard to resist.

It's the worst way to go, I think, but Fields kept his distance and foolish moves were totally out of the question. I started wondering who he would plug first.

We were on our stomachs, awaiting summary execution, when we heard the sounds of someone on the other side of the fire door. They knew the security code, and the door slowly swung open. To everyone's surprise, there stood T'zvi Pinsky in slippers and gray flannel pajamas, guiding himself with a thick, dark walking stick. He wore no sunglasses at the time, and for half an instant I rejoiced, believing that Ze'ev had once again arrived, machine gun in hand, to save my sorry hide. But hope faded fast.

"Chava, are you there?" asked T'zvi. His eyes stared blankly across the armory. "Who's here?"

"Step on in, you blind fool," ordered Fields. "I should've killed you right along with the others. No matter. Now it's—." He stopped suddenly in mid-sentence. I flinched as T'zvi raised the thick walking cane swiftly, pointing it directly at Fields.

A harsh, audible "Psssft!" erupted from the cane, and when I turned back towards Fields, a small, dark round hole appeared at the base of his throat, just above the top of his sternum. That same moment, blood began pouring from the entry wound. Field's expression changed from absolute shock to dim, swooning fear. His gun wavered in his trembling hands. He crumpled like a tower of blocks in a preschool classroom and never made a sound until his body hit the floor.

"Good shot, T'zvi!"

Chava leapt to her feet triumphantly and rushed over to Fields. I rolled to a knee and tried to stand, but could not. I still felt the pain of that pool cue slamming across my back from earlier. In fact, it seemed to hurt more than ever. I heard more footsteps at the door and looked up to see Charity and old man Temple entering the armory. I could not believe my eyes.

"Boss, are you okay?" Charity looked like a costumed commando, clad in a dark blue jumpsuit, a thick black belt and a matching blue beret. Her hair, dyed black, dangled behind her in a ponytail and as I stared at her in her strange garb she shrugged and said, "What?"

"You look...different."

"I know. I'm a hot brunette now. Get over it," she said impatiently. "Temple's here too. We followed you in this morning." They walked over, grabbed my arms on either side and stood me up. "Why is it that every time I catch up to you lately, you're on your butt? What's up with that?"

"I can't call it." I said. Despite their help, I felt strangely weak and wondered if the years might finally be catching up to me. "Just what the hell are you guys doing here? Forget it, tell me later..."

"Chava!" shouted T'zvi. "Everyone upstairs is dead! The whole team. In the computer room....everything's trashed, useless."

"That's impossible," said Chava.

"No, it's not. One of the kids found them. He said it's a bloody mess. None of the other kids are hurt, though. Most are still sleeping. I followed a hunch and came down here."

"I lose my team," said Chava, "and this asshole Fields is still alive? Not for long, though. I'm going to *San Jose* to kill that piece of shit *Vespula*—alone, if I have to!"

"You're not going in alone," I said.

"You're still in?"

"Of course. Just gear up." I turned to Charity. "It's Fields…your son's father, Charity…he turned I guess. I'm sorry. I'll explain it later. You better see to him. It doesn't look good…neck shot." Charity looked stricken. Despite their history, Fields was still her kid's dad, even if he was a sellout. She ran to him and kneeled down next to Chava. I could hear wet, gurgling sounds erupting from his throat. They tried stopping the rapid blood loss, but Fields had begun convulsing…I didn't think he had a chance in hell beyond a minute or two. Chava left his side and began gearing up quickly, as if he no longer mattered a bit. I looked once or twice at T'zvi Pinsky, who stood impassively in the middle of the room. I kept wondering about that cane shot that took out Fields, just how he pulled it off, but he acted as blind as everybody said he was. "You sure you can't really see out of one eye? That was one helluva hit."

"I aimed for the source of his voice, that's all. I don't know what would have happened if I missed. We'd probably all be dead now."

I stocked up on ammo and examined a sidearm while Temple filled me in on how he and Charity ended up in Costa Rica.

"After you left," said Temple, "Ze'ev Pinsky contacted us. You were already in flight to Costa Rica. Ze'ev told us the full specifics of *Vespula's* plan. If *Vespula* regains full access to his funds, he will use those financial resources to attack the United States."

"How?" I asked. "With another bomb? If *Mossad* had ever gotten their frigging act together and taken him out, we wouldn't even be having this conversation."

Right then, my mind was really more focused on picking out a good assault rifle than anything else. I settled on the best one present— a G36, made by a German company, Heckler Koch. It was light, plastic and fiberglass, and packed one hell of a punch. I'm not really a gun guy, but I do know what's called for when the time comes. If things got ugly in the jungles or the shanty town around *San Jose*, the G36 would serve nicely in helping me speak my mind. I had suffered enough near-deaths for one mission and I wasn't about to be subtle anymore. "If all it takes is a bullet to end this, I'll do it myself Temple."

"It's not that simple. I wish it were," said Temple. "You recall Maziar Safi?

"Yeah, the wrist blades guy with the talkative son. What of him?"

"And *Agua-Azul*..."

I remembered. "Some sort of water bottling company?"

"Yes, liquid storage tanks. Ze'ev Pinsky says Hezbollah has devised a plan to infect various water systems in the United States with a strain of bird virus...something akin to bird influenza, but worse."

"H5N1 can already mutate to infect humans," I said. "It's deadly, I think."

"Yes, quite right. You may have heard that our government told our researchers to take precautions to keep the virus from passing into terrorist hands. Well... too little, too late. Intelligence reports indicate that Hezbollah acquired a fast-mutating strain from a laboratory in the Netherlands...H5N2...the theft has been verified. It's a fast acting, military grade bio-weapon with no known vaccine...certain death in a matter of hours, unstoppable, a new weapon of mass destruction if delivered in liquid storage tanks and passed into the drinking water of several hub cities. That's where *Agua-Azul* comes in, a means of transport and delivery. Think of it...H5N2 could trigger a national catastrophe, perhaps even a worldwide epidemic. I've seen some footage of what the strain can do to a large colony of ferrets in a matter of days, Phillip. It's not pretty. *Vespula* is supposedly in possession, and *Aqua-Azul* is his game plan. That's why Ze'ev sent us, to warn you all. He couldn't risk relaying the information via phone or electronic communications, not something of this magnitude. All communications can be intercepted through the IT center upstairs, and we didn't know who the mole might be. I'm here to help you any way I can, brother man. Unfortunately, this rogue CIA agent, Fields, may have just wiped out our only means to stop *Vespula*, by killing off the entire team. I think the Chinese would call it, 'Beheading the Serpent in Its Lair.'

"That was his plan from Jump Street, Temple. I think I'd call it, 'We're Screwed, Man.' We're tactically crippled…very few options, now. Where is Ze'ev? Why isn't he here?"

"Ordered elsewhere, Honduras or Nicaragua I believe, to address an immediate national security matter…exact location unknown"

"Ordered by whom? He's out of *Mossad*. Who is *he* taking orders from now?"

"I don't know. Is this *Mossad* woman trustworthy?"

I wasn't quite sure how to answer, but I didn't have long to think about it.

"*Phillip!*" screamed Chava. Her tone said everything. I rushed over to a corner of the armory, where she stood, with Temple following close behind. "*Look.*"

I stared blankly for only an instant. "Temple… what?"

"What? You don't know a time bomb when you see one ticking?" said Temple. "Don't panic, though. Seven minutes left, plenty of time to clear the building. Just set off the fire alarms, perhaps?"

"We can't, Temple! Fields killed the alarms."

"Then we better work fast. That's PLX combined with C4, I think, and a lot of it. That much will blow a 757 out of the sky and not leave a trace of DNA."

"Deactivate it," I said.

"Can't, it's rigged. See here? And here? I can't stop it…nobody can in that amount of time." He looked over at Charity, still kneeling by the now lifeless body of Fields. "No help there, I'm afraid. He planned to kill everyone, and maybe let that guy *Vespula* claim the kill. What now…it's your call…or the *Mossad* lady's."

My instincts kicked in. "Okay then, everybody listen up! Temple, Charity and T'zvi, you're exiting out the back! Temple, it's your job to salvage what you can here first. Take…I don't know…whatever you think is usable. *Don't* overstay your welcome! T'zvi, you and Charity clear the alley and get to the next street…do whatever it takes to get people as far away as possible, and call the cops… Chava, we've got to get those kids upstairs out, you and I, and exit out the front before shit hits the fan...If Temple is right we're gonna have some big-ass fireworks in about five minutes...everybody *move!*"

It wasn't one of those last second escapes you see in movies. We got everybody out without a hitch. I even managed to save Spike in the process. But when that bomb went off, everything Temple left behind in the armory went up too. Half the building blew apart and lit up the whole night. No one took it harder than Chava. She was literally in tears.

"I lost it, everything. My people! The command post, all of it."

"Nobody else died," I said. "Fields lost, not us."

"My career is finished," she said. "What do I tell the agency? What do I tell Ze'ev."

"You tell them you exposed and silenced the leak to Hezbollah... that you suffered a big asset hit with maximum damage but limited your casualties to non-civilians. Your career is not over, not necessarily... not if we can stop *Vespula* before he kills anyone else. Your *Mossad* team is toast, but you still have me and Temple. We can be quite a handful, so quit whining and move on. Let's get the hell out of here before we all get arrested. The cops aren't exactly our allies right now...we can't trust a single one of them."

Temple urged us to use the old *Pinzgauer 101* all-terrain vehicle that he and Charity drove in coming to our rescue. "Mossad has been compromised," he reasoned crisply, "so that *Pinz* is the only vehicle I trust now!" It was a big, square-shaped thing, almost too stout and military-like to be discreet, but the monster had been painted white and disguised with decals to resemble a garbage truck.

"It's slow!" Chava objected. "It's too visible!"

"Don't argue with me! Get in the god-damn *Pinz* lady, you hear?" ordered Temple. I never heard him shout like that before. "Everybody move!" I briefly wondered in just what capacity he had served the CIA... he seemed a different man. Chava shut up and ran. He jabbed his finger at me as he sprinted with an armload of goods tucked under

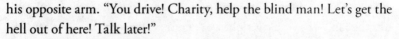

his opposite arm. "You drive! Charity, help the blind man! Let's get the hell out of here! Talk later!"

So that's what we did. As it happened, choosing the *Pinz* was a damn good decision too, because just after I turned the key in the ignition and the *Pinz's* turbo diesel engine roared to life... another explosion rocked us to the rafters.

The pickup truck that Chava Cresca drove, parked near the main entrance, went up as if a small warhead struck it dead center. It blew apart like a Matchbox car stuffed with a firecracker. The truck bed shot back, the rooftop flew up and the front end fire-balled right before our eyes. A heat wave enveloped the *Pinz* as we flinched and huddled, and then the rooftop crashed down to the street in front of us. I floored the *Pinz*, crushing the rooftop, and barreled forward as the smoke rose behind us.

"Damn! Double bomb, engine and gas tank," said Temple, as we sped away from the hot mess. "Agent Cresca, I think it's safe to say that Fields had all angles covered... I don't think he liked you very much either, by the way. Also Phillip, I'm monitoring police transmissions through this earplug I'm wearing. You're not going to believe this... they're already tagging this as a terrorist act by an American named Jerrod Singleton. They're saying you accidentally blew yourself up when the bomb went off."

"Wow. That was fast," I said.

"That's *Aguilera's* play," said Temple. "It had to be. Gotta say it, these guys are good...CIA-type coordination, timing and communications. They even blew the truck."

"Anticipating all avenues of escape," said Chava.

"Exactly," said Temple. "How long have you been at this, Agent Cresca? Phillip, you've never been under the radar...*never*. They always knew you were here, brother. I guess the only upside is that they think they got everybody, including you. We can use that to our advantage, but your cover name is blown to shit, too. You'll need a new passport..."

"Let's go," I said. "Now I'm really pissed off."

CHAPTER 20

It was two a.m. in the morning, and a hard rain had started falling on the road to *San Jose*. The *Pinz's* heavy wipers slapped intermittently, at times the only sound besides the pelting water on the windshield and roof. At other times I could hear *Anjela* talking softly in her native tongue, rapid and sure, as T'zvi pelted her with questions; but my mind was so preoccupied I caught nothing of what she said, and cared little. Her voice merged with all the other ambient sounds that mingled with the wheels turning inside my own head.

We made quite a motley crew, discreet and tense, perhaps a bit afraid even if we never actually said it...not exactly my idea of a crack rescue team. In fact, I had serious reservations about driving straight into a bloodbath— our own. We looked terribly conspicuous too, the six of us packed into a big monster ATV: myself driving, Chava fretting angrily, T'zvi brooding, Temple mentally inventorying our gear and monitoring radio frequencies, with Charity and *Anjela* along for the ride (and of course Spike, the least worried of the bunch, resting in young *Anjela's* warm lap). We couldn't go to the police or any government office, we didn't know who to trust. It seemed like everybody was in someone else's pocket. We saw several police units racing toward *Limon* as we raced away, and each time a cop car raced by I hoped they wouldn't think to wheel around and pursue us. Eventually, I got lucky and spotted a small convoy of six commercial SUV's— all packed with families heading into *San Jose*; I eased in behind them, hoping they would cover us all the way in. At that moment we needed all the cover we could get.

Chava had stripped Field's body, including his phone, his phony passport and his one way ticket to the Cook Islands. He had obviously banked on making his payday and disappearing, poor slime. Aww well, I thought, the greedy bastard entered life with nothing and left it holding the same, a most inglorious end befitting his bad intentions. His cell phone told us nothing useful... his contacts, whoever they might be, had used coded words which meant little to us. However, his Cook Islands plane flight was scheduled for noon the following day... so whatever business he planned completing after killing us all would have taken only a single day.

Temple began calculating our prospects.

"I have no idea exactly what we are headed for, but if my experience matters in such proceedings, I'd wager that wherever this banker Sabo is, we'll find a large contingent of gunmen surrounding the place, maybe a mix of cops and local bandits or drug cartel enforcers, and *Vespula's* hired help as well. As I see it, Sabo is alive because he has something they need, maybe an access code to all that money. They may have tortured him to within an inch of his life, but still, he has to know that if he talks...but then..."

He paused.

"What," I asked.

"Or maybe not... maybe no torture for him yet. Maybe they've brought in someone he would trust, perhaps a dear friend or family member...maybe his wife?"

"Or his daughter," I said. "At this point who knows?"

"Regardless," said Temple, "this man *Vespula* must be neutralized. He's too dangerous."

"That's an understatement, Temple," I said emphatically. "The guy will stop at nothing. If tonight doesn't prove that, I don't know what does."

My own mission had suddenly morphed into a dangerous venture

to protect America, or so it seemed. Inwardly, I hoped that all our suspicions were sound, that *Vespula* and *Aguilera* were in cahoots in some
twisted fashion, that they would meet at some point in the slums of *San
Jose* and that Sabo would be there too. It seemed too much to ask that
our slim intel was spot on, and that we'd get the drop on them, and
manage to ice *Vespula* and save Sabo in the process…even if I doubted
he was really worth saving. But that was the plan, the only one worth
pursuing, the only one that mattered anymore. Chava was right, I probably should have bailed out and not let my task-driven nature push me
on, but I am who I am.

"How are you doing back there, Charity," I asked. She had not
spoken since Fields had breathed his last at her knees. She seemed a
little shell-shocked.

"I'm okay."

"You sure?"

"Yeah. I just keep seeing his face. He looked scared at the very end.
I keep thinking he saw Hell or something. I know you don't believe
in it, but…"

"What, in spiritual Hell?" I asked. "No. Not the permanent fur-
nace they told me about in grade school. I do believe we do a good job
of making people suffer right here in this life. We do a damn good job
of that, don't we?"

Nobody answered. We rumbled steadily along in our adopted
mini-convoy. Chava had not spoken for some time. I wondered if
she felt angry or defeated by Temple's verbal shellacking; it was
hard to tell. I looked out ahead and watched the rain pelting the
windshield, noting how it made things shimmer quite eerily. I
caught my secretary's eyes in the big rearview mirror as she sat in
the back seat.

"What, boss," she asked.

"Just thinking, Charity. There's an old Buddhist saying… 'When
you're born, you cry, and the world rejoices. When you die, you rejoice,
and the world cries…' I don't think that your ex, Mr. Fields, rejoiced

at the end. I don't think anybody mourned either, not even you that much. Maybe going out like that is a kind of hell in itself?"

"Hey, Teacher," said Temple, "We just picked up company."

"What have we got?" I asked. I saw two headlights in the side mirror, moving up in the pouring rain. "Police car?"

"Two motorcycles creeping up. I think they went by the other way and then turned around… coming up faster now. Don't panic yet, it could be nothing."

"Of course." I didn't have to tell anyone not to look around… the *Pinz* had only a 'peek-a-boo' rear window, about the size of a clipboard. It had also been modified with two sets of side mirrors, a large set on the front doors and a small set for rear-door passengers, which enabled Temple to stay on the watch discreetly. I stayed cool and quietly closed the distance between us and the traveling convoy of SUV's… I wanted to look like part of the group. The bikers swept up behind us like they owned the rode and stayed tight. I did not like it. I maintained a steady speed and kept my contact with the traveling convoy and nothing happened for about three miles.

"I'm listening. They have not utilized their radios yet," said Temple, "and I think they would have by now if they had a legitimate concern." He had barely finished his sentence when one of the bikes flashed a bright blue strobe light and beeped. It sounded like a courteous beep, short and sharp. "Great…I jinxed us," said Temple.

I glanced quickly over my shoulder at him. He sighed and removed his headphones. "I'll fix this, my man. Maintain current speed and course." He clambered over the rear passenger seat and into the cargo area. *Anjela* followed, and before Temple said anything, she had peeked out the little back window. She whispered at length to Temple, who followed up with, "*Anjela* says they are not police motorcycles."

"How does she know that," Chava asked, before I could ask myself.

"She says they are *Carabela* GS3's, manufactured in Mexico… used by enforcers for the *Sinaloa* drug cartel… she knows the make and model from the three front lights and the side view mirrors. She saw that bike model all the time back when she knew *Vespula*."

"Wow, what a touching memory," said Charity. "Maybe they want to be friends with us too..."

"Not in this life I bet," said Temple. The motorcycles both beeped again. "They're potential hostiles. So what do you want me to do... assault rifle or dazzler rifle?"

"Let's not be too hasty," I said. But then one of the bikers accelerated, pulled up alongside us, flashed a shiny badge and motioned for us to pull over. As he dropped back behind us I saw the *Carabela* logo splashed across his gas tank and knew young *Anjela* was spot on. I also saw a fully-kitted Ruger SR-15 strapped across his back. "Do *Fuerza Publica* guys carry SR-15's, Chava?"

"Not in this life," she said echoing Temple. "Better lose 'em or bruise 'em..." About that moment we hit a stormy patch. Rain began pelting us hard. The stretch of road ahead narrowed with a small rise, the kind that dips quickly on the other side and blocks the oncoming view. The convoy of SUV's sped on before us. Chava must have known what I was thinking. "If you are going to do it, do it now..."

I switched to the opposing lane and floored the *Pinz*. Despite its bulk it had quickness and speed. "Temple, do what you gotta do," I said, and made my run for the front of the pack. The motorcycles whipped out right behind us, almost anticipating our move. They made the *Pinz* seem like it was standing still, and we were only halfway past the convoy when I saw light glowing beyond the coming rise. A spray of gunfire burst forth from the lead bike and the road beside us erupted with fury. He was herding me strong right, but I really had nowhere to go. The convoy limited my options. So I stepped on the gas pedal as hard as I could and drove straight ahead.

Temple flipped open the little back window. "You might want to keep looking forward, everybody. I've never used a dazzler rifle before." A sudden flickering of strange green light filled the *Pinz*. In my side mirror, I saw the lead bike swerve violently, and another hail of gunfire tore wildly from the SR15, into the convoy. All the vehicles reacted to the gunfire and one big SUV swerved into the path of the lead bike. "It hit him… it hit him!" cried Temple, "He spun out… oh, he's frigging toast… that's all she wrote."

I swung back into my own lane just as we hit the rise, and a big, silver *Dos Pinos* milk truck with a bright green logo came barreling through. It barely missed us, and our windshield went totally wet-gray from the road spray. For half a second we were blind. I had absolutely no idea what happened when that Milk truck blew through that traveling convoy. We didn't stop.

"What happened to the other biker," I asked, finally.

"I saw him swing hard right," said Charity. "He went behind the convoy. I don't know what happened after that. That dazzler thing works, though."

"You're not going to believe this…" said Temple. He was looking out the little back window. "The other one's coming up now."

"I don't see anything…" I said.

"You can't," said Temple. "He's off the road on the far right shoulder, way back coming slowly, along the tree line. It's rough terrain and he's all over the place, but he's coming. He's hanging back, deliberately staying out of my sightline, but he'll catch us eventually even in this weather. I can't believe the son of a gun made it through all that!"

"I can't believe he didn't turn back," said Chava. "How far back is he now?"

"I'd say seven hundred yards, maybe less."

"Hand me that assault rifle," said Chava. "Stop, Phillip."

I stepped off the gas pedal and broke speed as fast as I safely could. Before we fully stopped, Chava jumped from her seat, hit the pavement with both feet and raised the Heckler Koch assault rifle as coolly as an old sailor with a brass telescope. I quickly moved to Chava's passenger seat so I could lean out of her door and track her shot. The *Carabela* had already closed the distance. I saw the rider reach over his shoulder and begin to bring his SR-15 round front to take aim. Chava fired one time. His helmet flew off like half a bowling ball when it separated from his head. The bike's front wheel twisted violently. Machine and man went into a wild, tumbling somersault. Parts flew everywhere. Then everything came to rest. The sound of the rain took over again. I returned to my seat and Chava climbed back aboard.

"Hope the people in that convoy are okay," I said, "and the milk trucker, too. Bet he was a family man."

CHAPTER 21

I had no intention of allowing Charity or T'zvi to continue on with us after that. I decided to drop them both off at the first two-story hotel we passed on the road. It happened to be a colorfully painted, Mayan-themed little place called *Uchuch Q'uq'* in a town called *La Verdad* (translation: The Truth). Don't ask me how to pronounce the hotel, I've long since forgotten, but I do remember T'zvi saying that it meant 'Green-feathered Mother' in the old Mayan tongue.

"Oh, '*H*' to the '*ell*' frickin' no!"

That's what Charity shouted as soon as I drove the *Pinz* into the *Uchuch Q'uq'* parking lot. I guess she knew what I had in mind.

"Come on Boss…*really*? I'm flopping out in *there* while you guys ride off into the night to save the frickin' world? That's why I flew all the way down here, so you could drop me off like some loser and sit around until you guys get your man? That's not cool…"

"It's too dangerous," said Temple. "You've done all you can."

"Think again," said Charity. "I'm just getting started. Dangerous? You guys don't know what dangerous is. Stick one of those guns in my hands, I'll show you dangerous. I happen to be a pretty good shot too."

"Charity, this isn't target practice at a gun range," I said. "We're going into a kill zone. People shoot back. Get out of the *Pinz*. That's an order." I wasn't messing around. "Chava, what about *Anjela*?"

"That's your call, since you've taken up making them. We could use her if she knows her way around that shanty town, and dump her off once we get to ground zero. But as for T'zvi, and your feisty little office girl… they're definite liabilities."

Charity fumed "Office girl? And what are you, the boot camp girl? Look Sweets, I'm not scared. I know the risks because every time I leave my Boss to his own means, he ends up getting halfway killed. If it wasn't for me and Ze'ev and Dr. Temple he'd be dead twice already, do you even realize that? My son's father is dead, I almost got blown up and you guys still don't think I'm qualified to risk my life for my country! This asshole *Vespula*, whoever he is, is trying to poison everybody in America. If he gets away from us he just might pull it off. But I'm supposed to play the helpless —what did you call me?— office girl? Forget about that…"

"We don't have time to argue," said Temple. "It's counterproductive. She understands the danger, Phillip. When you were kidnapped and being eaten alive by Conga Ants, she came with Ze'ev to save you, and she got you to me. Tonight she risked her life for you again, and watched her child's father die in her arms. She knows the risks because she's taken them for you. As for this other young girl, *Anjela*, if you want to drop her off, fine, but from what I've gathered in the brief time I've been aboard, she knows the city and that shanty town *Los Guido* better than all of us. I'm not even sure we can find the place before the *Fuerza Publica* nabs us, and if we fall into their hands, given *Aguilera's* power and influence we might *all* get shot, the same way her brother was."

I nodded. "And you know all this about her brother… how?"

"Well, Charity filled me in on the way over, that's part of it… and among my many talents I happen to speak very good Spanish, my man. You don't. But everyone else in this car does, and this young lady *Anjela* happens to be a very good story teller. She's filled us in on quite a bit.

"That's all well and good." I conceded. "But as for you, Charity, you're staying here. You too, T'zvi. Go check in."

"I'll need my notebook, Temple," muttered Charity. "Crap, if I can't partake I might as well play online Scrabble. Lag sucks of course, with all the weak Sat signals, and the ping is dreadful, but what's a gal to do when she's told to sit one out?"

She was being sarcastic. Everybody knew.

"I think I'm paying you to be more productive than that," I said.

"Hardly," she protested. "I don't have any money to check us in. No plastic either. T'zvi probably has just the clothes on his back."

"Not true," said T'zvi. "I also have my cane, but nothing more."

"Fine, I'll check you both in then." I stepped out of the car. "Let's go."

I covered their check-in and escorted them to their room. Charity was silent and piss-angry the whole time. Once we entered the seedy hotel flat she opened her mouth to protest again but I silenced her with a look. I took my watch off and handed it to her.

"Now that we're alone...here, take this. Ze'ev can locate you both with it, just like he did me. T'zvi, there's got to be a way for you or Charity to contact him."

"Maybe," said T'zvi. "If Charity can tap into a satellite..."

"You've got to, Charity, you've done it before... if you succeed, Ze'ev can rendezvous with you. You can follow his lead. That's the best plan, since you're bucking my authority. You'll also have to make arrangements for us to get back to the States, non-traditional means, and at a moment's notice if necessary. That is, if it doesn't interfere with your online gaming. I'm counting on you. Can you do that?"

"Of course I can, what did you hire me for? Have I ever let you down yet? *No.* I'm not bucking authority. I just don't understand the plan..."

"I know, no one does."

"You guys are making it up as you go along?" said Charity.

"Maybe so. Whole wars get fought that way, lately. But I had to pull you two away from the others."

"Why?" asked T'zvi.

"Because it's getting too dangerous from here on out. Because with everything at stake, and all that money… let's just say I smell a rat. Trust…that's issue number one for me. I trust you of course, Charity. Temple… he's clean… I've known him too long to think otherwise… and as for you T'zvi, I know you've got Ze'ev's back. He's always had yours."

"Of course…"

"That leaves Chava," I said. "She's really the unknown quantity. That banker, Sabo, he's the key to over a hundred million dollars. Your hubby was slime, Charity, but he couldn't act alone."

T'zvi frowned. "Chava? Never! She has been rather quiet, sure. She hasn't been herself since we escaped that hellfire. It's not like her to withdraw, but she would *never* betray us for money. She just wouldn't…"

"Well, call me overcautious if you want, but I can't completely trust anyone. A mistake like that could get us all killed. All this happened on her watch. At the very least she's suspect… don't you think? So in effect, I've split us up… just in case. That's why I need you to contact Ze'ev any way you can, T'zvi. If everything goes south, you two might be my only chance of getting out of *Los Guido* alive. I've got to get back." I handed Charity a small caliber handgun I had tucked in my waistband. "It's just a little 32 Tomcat but it'll do some damage. We practiced with it a while back, remember? Don't be shy with it, and keep the door locked."

Charity nodded. "I knew you trusted me…and like always I won't let you down." Looking into her eyes, I suddenly realized she cared a lot more about me than she ever let on. "Did you and this Chava Cresca… become friends?"

"Yeah. But it was strictly professional…"

Charity shrugged and glanced toward T'zvi, who acted mildly self-conscious. "I bet. Sorry, Boss…it's none of my business. She's… I just figured as much, that's all…"

"Look, it's all in the game. I gotta get back, time's flying."

"I just hope Ze'ev gets here in time…" said Charity.

"You'll hear from him, I'm sure of that. By the way, you look tougher with the dark hair. And remember… I'm counting on you Charity, so do your thing. See you after *Los Guido*, hopefully."

CHAPTER 22

When I came back, the rain had subsided to a faint drizzle. Chava and Temple were standing outside the vehicle with *Anjela* still sitting in the back seat, invisible due to the tinted black windows and a satiny curtain of tiny raindrops coating the glass.

We discussed our weapons. I admired how Temple did his best under potentially life-shortening duress.

"Thanks, Phillip. That armory was something else, all kinds of killing things, lots of American rifles, Israeli handguns...but really... most of it was no good to us. Just my gut feeling," said Temple, "especially given the frustrating reality that we are not octopuses with opposable thumbs, and right now...we are on our own, unquestionably."

"Ze'ev's contacts..." I suggested. "His people on the front end..."

"No go, Mr. Specialist," said Temple. "We've spent the better part of an hour trying to make contact with *San Jose*... all known secure channels... no response... I even tried every digital method I can think of ...no luck."

"How can that happen," I asked, looking too Chava. "Don't you have somebody... *anybody?*" She frowned and shook her head quietly, but offered nothing.

"It's all dead space out there," bemoaned Temple, handing each of us an earpiece with Secret Service style acoustic coil tubes. "From now on we may be talking to each other, but that's about it. Better assume that any help we might have had is in the wind, that they all

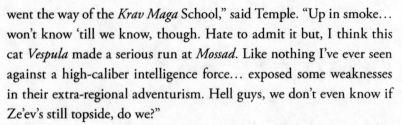

went the way of the *Krav Maga* School," said Temple. "Up in smoke…
won't know 'till we know, though. Hate to admit it but, I think this
cat *Vespula* made a serious run at *Mossad*. Like nothing I've ever seen
against a high-caliber intelligence force… exposed some weaknesses
in their extra-regional adventurism. Hell guys, we don't even know if
Ze'ev's still topside, do we?"

"Don't be ridiculous," said Chava. "Of course he's alive."

Like me, she simply disavowed the prospect, although the chilling
thought circled back, vulture-like, to haggle with my certainty. I felt
the rain increase slightly as my mind waved off the unthinkable. "It all
stinks of an internal betrayal," I admitted finally, "but I'm not worried.
Ze'ev will do what Ze'ev does."

"Sorry," said Temple, "didn't mean to play spoiler. On a good
note Chava, I did manage to grab two *SMU100's* and whole crate of
XM84's."

"Excellent," said Chava. "The dazzler rifle is incredible. I'm not sure
how effective it will be as we go forward, but I'm glad you thought to
bring two. It sure put a hurting on that biker."

"So did you! I have never seen a kill quite like that one. Nice head
shot. By the way, the *SMU100's* are intended as non-lethal weapons,
Phillip… I took that into consideration. I should have considered the
consequences given the weather and traffic conditions. Obviously I
exacerbated the crisis. In this case, the SMU100 proved lethal. My
apologies."

The *SMU100's* were powerful laser rifles designed to temporarily
blind attackers. At distance, they could devastate a tight group of men
or render an open doorway impassible with open eyes— not wise in a
firefight with *Mossad* or anybody else for that matter. At that time, the
SMU100 laser rifles were new on the scene… there was a lot of talk
about what they could or could not do. The Brits had started using
them tactically, and a rumor surfaced that a top secret version of the
rifles could fry your eyes permanently. No one knew much about them
at the time, but they were wicked scary, and that made them a powerful

intimidation tool. I do know that once a few Somali pirates got a taste, it severely hampered their appetite for high seas shenanigans.

The *XM84's* were military stun grenades but had the unique feature of separate 'flash' and 'bang' charges, increasing their tactical value immensely.

"...Oh...and I'm not sure what hunting shops Ze'ev frequents," said Temple, "but there's two twelve gauge shotguns and boxes of *Thor's Thunder* ammo. I've always liked the ring of that... *Thor's Thunder*... very descriptive, you know. They could prove useful too...are you familiar?"

"I think so." I said. "Bright, blinding flash, huge boom, no slugs? Military grade..."

"Yeah... a SWAT team's calling card," said Temple. "Or, as they say in hunting circles, *bear chasers*. Two hundred decibels of boom, two million candles of flash and two atmospheric pressures of concussion at close-range ...marvelous things...they'll wake the snorting citizens halfway back to *Limon*...but they won't kill anybody. Too bad."

"I'm still hoping to avoid that." I was the odd thinker.

"Well, good luck," said Chava, sounding more bitter than sarcastic. "The chances of me getting *Vespula* without some blood splatter are practically *nil*. And all that non-lethal stuff doesn't count for much when it escalates. We need boots on the ground. We lost those in *Limon*. Our objectives are partly related, Phillip, but my desired outcome is totally opposed to yours. And the people standing in our way... newsflash, they've got guns and they're stone cold killers. That's all I need to know. Preserve life when the target is threatening your country, your fellow citizens... for what? Never saw that concept in a training manual. Kung Fu them and flash-bang them all you want. I'm aiming to hurt somebody, and at this point that includes anybody that gets in my way."

"We've all got guns, Chava," I said. "We all know how to use them. Maybe you are right. We don't have boots on the ground. I *was* counting on that. Any plan to replace the men you've lost or the one's we can't contact now will take time—time we don't have. The window is closing, I know that much. But I still want to see what we're facing with my own eyes. Maybe we'll have to huff and puff and blow the whole house down, but we won't know till we get there. *Anjela* can get us there, to *The Hole*. She grew up in *Los Guido*. She might even help us avoid a pitfall or two, right?"

"Fine. Let's roll... I so hate the rain."

Temple raised a hand. "Our best bet is not to enter *Los Guido* on wheels. We are better off getting close and going on foot. I like our chances a whole lot better that way... that *Pinz* has got a big, loud footprint..."

CHAPTER 23

"Welcome to the sleepy township of *Guatuso*," Temple said blandly, as if already weary of the hunt. "The *Los Guido* shanty is straight ahead, a little over a mile. Angela says this is where we should stop, otherwise we'll pick up the eyes and ears of the locals on the last leg. And we don't want that. There's a wooded area, perhaps two hundred yards wide, running the length of *Los Guido* to the north, and we can travel through that scrub to avoid detection and get to *The Hole*. We need to get fully prepared before we go any further, though. *Anjela* says there's an old abandoned *casabuelo* on a hill nearby. It lies in a small patch of jungle and can link us to the larger patch bordering *Los Guido*. From the *casabuelo*, we'll have to cross a dirt road, cut through the jungle and then cross the corner of a small farm... maybe cut some wire or hop a wooden fence, but nothing serious. She says the *casabuelo* is very well hidden. We can park in the rear and no one will ever see the *Pinz*."

"If you don't mind me asking," I said, 'what's a... *casabuelo*?"

"Well," said Temple, "literally... it means 'grandpa's house,' but I guess the best definition is 'spirit home of the elders.' It doesn't have to be a relative's home. It just means old and small. *Guatuso* is the name of the township, but it's also the name of a tribe and the language they speak. There are fewer than a thousand of that tribe left now. They built these *casabuelo's* a long time ago, and now the builders are old men... grandpa's. Get it?"

"Got it," I said.

"The *Guatuso* tribe, the older ones anyway," said Temple, "believe that a *casabuelo* holds special power. They're the places where ancestral spirits dwell. That thinking has faded in these modern times, but old legends die hard."

"Interesting concept," I said.

It was perfect, from the outside, anyway.

Several small palms flanked the little home, with rough clumps of green cover thoroughly obscuring the front. A constant, misty drizzle had settled in, which lent a strange gloominess to the place. A grassy pathway, muddy and lumpy but still wide enough for the *Pinzgauer*, rolled to the rear. We cut the headlights, parked the *Pinz* and unloaded our gear. Of course we cleared the place before settling in, and then, while Temple and Chava sorted through things, I clambered up an old rickety ladder which leaned against the *casabuelo's* back wall and mounted the low-slung, flat tar roof.

I took a look around, ignoring the wet weather. The night was black. The silvery glow of *San Jose's* many lights shimmered off the dark northern skies. To the west, a fainter glow indicated the location of *Los Guido,* perhaps a twenty minute hike through the dense, high scrub. The weather and the terrain still favored us, and that sat well with me.

"Phillip, where are you?" Chava's voice erupted inside my earphone.

"Up on the roof, just like the old song says… checking things out. Just how abandoned is this place? What's your impression?"

"Some foot traffic. Little feet, mostly sneakers…kids come here. It's a mess. I see some evidence of drinking and drugs in the back but nothing too recent. I suggest we move the *Pinz* back deeper in the bushes before we leave, just to be on the safe side. See anything?

"No. Seems good. You guys ready?"

"We'll be ready when you are. Spike's looking for you."

But I didn't leave right away. I simply stood there atop the roof. I was completely exhausted. In fact, I had never been so tired in my whole life, nor more doubtful. I had returned to Costa Rica, and now my prior failure seemed set to repeat itself, poised to make my internal defeat utterly complete...and as I stood, weary beyond description, far too weary, I did something I had not done in as long as I could remember. I knelt down upon my knees.

Not to pray, as feeble men do when feeling desperate and forlorn. Such piety seldom works in my world, not when fate conspires against you and nature herself declines to oblige.

But kneel I did, tired and sore and hoping for relief, eager for a sign... a good omen. I meditated in the most unlikely of settings... on the old tar rooftop with a drizzle coating my face... my mind absorbed... seeking an inner sanctum lying dormant at my inner core. I had traveled that path before and found a gateway when I needed to.

And then, behind a misty curtain, as I blocked out the faint rustle of a bird's dampened wings and the sounds of human movement below, it happened...

I was gone, just part of the mist, a shadowy minion of darkness, a receptive vessel.

I felt the gloom softened by the rising sun of faint dawns yet un-born, though in truth pitch darkness still reigned... Still, the warmth, the light, the wind rustling in the trees all seemed so real.

I looked up, not certain if I had actually done so. Were my eyes open, or still closed in my meditative state? I wondered.

A Resplendent *Quetzal* sat majestically on a branch above me. It stared down, bright and green and magnificent, with a breast as scarlet as newly spilled blood. A flash of fine green hair crowned its noble head like a Roman crest. It called, subtle in its confidence, proud like the Aztec kings who once ruled and held it in so high regard.

And then his voice whispered...an old voice... wise... distant perhaps... *Do not fear the Great Ones, the ones who stare out from high perches...* and as the voice faded a roll of thunder, faint yet weighty, tumbled across the pre-dawn horizon.

I stared at the *Quetzal*... and suddenly, a small powerful owl glided in and struck like lightning....

With a cry of fear and protest the crested *Quetzal* recoiled desperately in a flurry of feathers, barely avoiding the raptor's grasp. It then fluttered away hurriedly into the rain as the owl screeched, flapping its own silent wings of death. A single long, green tail feather floated down, twisting like a maple seed. It landed near my left hand... and the voice returned... *You will prevail in all things...* It felt like a dream.

I somehow lost time. I felt a wondrous, calm sense of satisfaction and relief. I did not want to move... did not want to disturb that moment... even as the misty rain continued to fall... I reached for the fallen feather.

"Phillip..." Out of nowhere, her hand touched my shoulder.

"Yes Chava..."

"Is your earphone working? We tried reaching you... You did not answer and... I'm sorry, I didn't mean to..."

"It's all right, Chava... you didn't... I'm good." I rose to my feet. "Something odd occurred. If I tell you... you'll think I'm mad."

"No... tell me. I want to know... You see, when you did not answer us, I was going to climb the ladder... but I didn't."

"Really?"

"Yes, really... Temple tried to reach you first and then me. Spike was running around, looking for you, and his ear flipped up, Phillip, and it stayed up. You know, sort of across the top of his head... and we laughed... but then Temple saw a tattoo in Spike's ear. It was a tattoo of a wasp with the word *Vespula* beneath the wasp... We think the dog may have belonged to our *Vespula*, Phillip! Angela knows the owner by face. He left that dog with her."

"Was he from England? *Vespula* worked for the Brits."

"Yes! That's what I was going to tell you! Spike is actually a black and tan British Terrier. It all adds up. And so I came... but when I touched the ladder...I sort of froze, I hesitated...I don't know why...it's like I knew I must wait...and then the feeling went away and I came up here...and there you were...so please, tell me what happened. I won't think anything."

"Chava...I believe I was visited by the spirit of my great-grand-father...just now. I believe that because it's happened before... spirit traces from long ago...he was a native American...he told me we will win, Chava..."

She looked at me strangely, as if she had broken her word and really did think me mad... then finally she asked, "Are you are sure you are okay? I don't think anything bad, but..."

I nodded, certain within myself. "Don't worry. I'm good. Trust me." She moved her lips to speak but I raised a finger to freeze them. "Do you have a flashlight, Chava?"

"Yes..."

"Shine it in that palm tree... carefully please." She did, cautiously, and on a palm branch sat a bright crested Resplendent *Quetzal*. "Don't ask me how I knew it would be there," I said softly. "I just knew." The large green bird huddled on a dripping branch, looking dour and determined in the darkness. One of its long, glorious tail feathers had fallen away. Its dark, beadlike eyes shifted fleetingly from the flashlight beam and glanced toward the black skies above us. Chava turned the flashlight toward me. "Before tonight ends, that bird will have to fly for its life, Chava, from an owl. I saw it happen already." I raised my hand and held up a single, long green tail feather. "The Aztecs believed these feathers had power. Only the royalty could wear them, on pain of death. And the Cherokee, my great-grandfather's tribe, believed that all magical feathers had to be found by chance and not by killing, just like this one. Feathers have always been special to me. This one has a meaning too...everything will be okay, Chava... so let's go." We climbed down the ladder and entered the *casabuelo*.

"Good news," said Temple, as we entered the old house. "Ze'ev made contact. He is on his way to *San Jose* now. We are to move ahead and conduct recon of *The Hole*. His men located *Vespula* and were shadowing his entourage closely, but then every man went silent...no trace, and that's not good, but we're still in business, Phillip. We are close. We are going to finally get this guy."

"I know," I said. "How did Ze'ev contact us?"

"Charity's notebook, initially," said Temple. "No online Scrabble for her after all, I assume. You must have given her some type of pep talk."

"Charity never stays mad at me for long, Temple."

"We now have our own line," said Temple, handing me a plastic credit card, barely thicker than the real thing. "Flex it quickly twice. It'll beep once. Then just wait. Talk into it like a cell phone. It's secure."

I had never seen one like it before. "Where'd you get this?"

"I make them for the CIA. They work in ATM's, they record audio and they take photos, too. I call them 'calling cards.' Clever, yes?"

"Positively adroit," I said dryly. "Is it secure? Really secure?"

"Don't insult me, brother man… digital encryption, with my own customizable crypto-algorithm. Flex it. Ze'ev will be expecting you. It would be rude to keep him waiting…"

I flexed the card. Ze'ev answered immediately.

"Well, glad to see you've not been permanently impaired," he said. I was impressed by the calling card's sound clarity. "You made quite a smash in *Limon* I hear," he added, chuckling softly.

"Where have you been hiding?"

"Hardly hiding… northern Nicaragua, my friend… the municipality of *Murra* to be specific."

"What sent you there?"

"I heard that Nicaragua's *Dipilto* coffee —made the Persian way— is far bolder than any of the Costa Rican offerings. So I went to see for myself."

"And what did you find?"

"I found exactly what I was looking for at one place in particular."

"Will you be staying a while?"

"No. Unfortunately, the place went out of business

—permanently— shortly after my arrival. There was an explosion and a terrible fire. The owner and several of his employees perished. They were independently-minded Iranian entrepreneurs and very well-liked by the local people. Pity."

He had destroyed another Hezbollah nest. "Indeed... and what now?"

"There is a small *casabuelo* with a beautiful view of *San Jose*," said Ze'ev. "I plan to travel there and relax a bit. You should proceed as planned. I'm sorry my other friends have not contacted you yet. They certainly knew you were traveling through the area. It's not like them at all, and unless something drastic happened, it's inexcusable. I feel slighted. I will surely have a few words with them about it. I hate when trusted friends let me down."

"I have a confession to make then," I said. "I loved that costly watch you gave me as a gift, but I was so moved by local poverty that I donated it to charity. I hope you understand."

"It was a fine thing to do. I appreciate your honesty. I am not offended at all. Don't fret. I will see you soon enough. Take care."

"Farewell." I looked at Temple. "Leave a homing device in the *Pinzgauer* for Ze'ev. There's also been some trouble. The *Limon* agents were not the only ones hit... something's afoot with the ones stationed here in *San Jose*, too. Ze'ev has been keeping very busy."

"Yes," said Temple. "and now it's our turn."

CHAPTER 24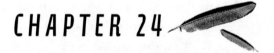

Anjela led us on a dirt path heading to *Los Guido*, clutching Spike to her breast as we waked single file, close to the brush. We had to stay off the main dirt roads. Her family lived in the heart of the shanty town, where the gangs battled for the tiny drug turf and the street girls made their money, and everyone knew her.

Eventually we hit a fence line that ran the entire northern length of the *Los Guido* slum, with *The Hole* lying ahead on the far western end, surrounded by coconut palms, strangler vines and various other shrubs. We were actually walking through jungle, and we could barely see each other's faces from the small bit of light filtering in from *Los Guido*.

We all assumed *Anjela* might desire to break off at some point, slip through the fencing, and return home, leaving us to our business. However, when it came down to it, she begged off. At a gaping hole in the fence, she simply turned to me and whispered, "Me no go back." Then she looked at Temple and pleaded in Spanish.

"She says there's nothing there for her," said Temple.

"Why not?" I asked.

"*Aguilera* killed her brother and then *Vespula* used her and passed her off to a drug dealer," said Temple. "She's marked as a cartel whore now, and it's permanent. Her parents work for a Christian Mission... the New Life Church. The church tore down their house and helped to build them a new one. Her parents don't want her there. It will ruin their reputation with the local minister, they think. They told her to never come back. That's what she says, Phillip."

"She'll get killed," warned Chava. "She can't come with us. No way. Let her find another path to redemption… *this* road is closed."

Temple listened to *Anjela* again. "She's not afraid to die."

"Me no go back," insisted *Anjela*. "Me go USA… good place."

"Tell her *no*," insisted Chava. "We've helped her enough. It's stupid to expect more. We can find *The Hole* from here."

"Me no go back… *Voy a luchar por ti*… Me fight for you…"

"Don't just toss her aside, Chava," I said. "She saw you kick ass and take names at that bar. Now she wants to be like you."

"I'm not here to play big sister. You are not here to play big brother. Temple is not here to play daddy…"

Chava had a point. I felt for *Anjela*, sure. The fact that Spike was *Vespula's* dog, and that he left Spike behind with *Anjela*, and that we in turn stumbled across her seemed almost too coincidental, the stuff of storybooks, but it had happened. Sometimes things happen for a reason. Still, she didn't belong with us. Yes, she could positively identify *Vespula*, but could I live with myself if I got her killed, just like her brother Rico Bravo… no, I couldn't. But if I made her hop the fence and go home, I had no control over who she talked to or what she told them…and what about *Vespula*? What did he look like? It was a tough choice. But one thing seemed certain: *Anjela* had spunk.

"You fight for me, now me fight for you… Me no go back, *si?*"

"Tell her she's still on the team, Temple," I said. "She knows *Vespula*."

"*No*," said Chava, instantly. "It endangers the mission. Tell her to go back to the *casabuelo,* Temple. Tell her to wait for us. Tell her we won't leave her behind… that we promise to come back for her."

Temple grabbed his cap by the brim and whipped water off to the side before replacing it upon his head. "You tell her that."

Chava hissed orders in Spanish. *Anjela* fired back a response.

Temple shook his head. "She doesn't believe you..."

Chava glared, put her fist in the younger woman's face and punched it hard into her opposite hand, then pointed back down the trail. *"No discutas conmigo... Volver, Anjela!"*

Crushed, but too proud to cry, *Anjela* clutched Spike to her chest and turned around. But before she left she looked at me one last time and asked, "Why me go back? ...Why me no fight for *you?*"

"Stay..." It was not pity. It was a tactical decision.

"I told her to go back," said Chava, "but you want to clash with me... really? Okay, Mr. Specialist, do it your way. Run your little rescue mission. You play great leader... but decisions like that can come back to bite your ass... just so you know."

Temple seemed neutral. "If she can finger *Vespula* it's worth the risk."

I felt right about it. Ze'ev would have done the same. We all knew that. Chava had lost her people in *Limon*, I reasoned... maybe that was eating at her, or maybe she actually had a soft spot for *Anjela* and she only knew one way to show it.

Either way we crept on, and as we trekked, the somber skies wept.

———

Los Guido is not a district that became a slum, but rather a slum that became a district. It started as a squatter's town on public land. The squatters built shelters out of whatever scraps they could beg, barter or pinch. Once they built the shelters and suffered no legal consequences, more squatters moved in. So then the squatter town became a shanty town thirty thousand strong, and the dirt roads got paved. Soon, real homes got built. After that, power lines went up and streetlights came on. So the shanty town grew more... fifty thousand strong. That's when churches and gangs grew prevalent... maybe to give people something 'really real' to live and die for. So

that's how *Los Guido* came to be… that's how it became 'a district.'
Some folks would call that progress, but a lot of old-timers confess
that they liked it better when *Los Guido* was just a slum.

———

We were well-concealed, voice connected and in triangulated
viewing positions long before first light. We soon realized that the
security perimeter guarding *The Hole* consisted of a skeleton crew that
became fully expanded at dawn. At that time, a *Fuerza Publica* unit
rolled in with four vans and four small motorcycles. Supposedly, they
were Counter Narco-Terrorism Operatives specially trained by the
US Military at Fort Benning. They all wore ballistic vests over their
black *Policia* jumpsuits and toted around high-end assault rifles like
they knew how to use them. They also wore hooded ski masks called
balaclavas. Chava said the *balaclavas* hid their faces from the cartels,
if they ever did real police work, which seemed unlikely. It looked to
us like these operatives protected the bad guys. They didn't do much
after arriving. They stood around talking and neglected to check their
perimeter, where we lay unseen. They seemed slack. Temple intercepted
transmissions about an 'anti-narcotics sweep' which we disregarded as
cover noise. They were *not* there fighting crime. We minimized our own
chatter and just watched their movement patterns.

From my vantage point, I could survey the natural depression
lengthwise. *The Hole* reminded me of a natural amphitheater, like the
Hollywood Bowl in miniature. A colossal *kapok* tree dominated the
center, two-hundred feet high, spreading its immense branches like an
overarching pavilion. Everything else lay in its benevolent shadow.

Three makeshift housing structures had been built by the original
squatters, two made of sheet metal and a third made of wood. Sandbag
walls now surrounded each one. Based on post-dawn activity we concluded that someone was held captive in the wooden structure. The
sheet metal structures served some other use.

"This is odd," I finally said into the ears of the others. "No FARC forces, no *Vespula*, just locals."

"Just because you can't see them," a new voice said in my ear, "doesn't mean they aren't there."

I nodded. "Ze'ev... glad you could make it. Temple said this channel---"

"Don't fret, it's a secure channel. We are private."

"What's the story..."

"Target is enroute to you now. Target is in the air."

"Clarify, Ze'ev..."

"Two AH6 helicopters... capable birds... armed ...Browning heavy machine guns... four snipers... Do not engage while in the air... Copy?"

"Copy."

"Here is something else you should know," said Ze'ev. "The U.S. currently has seven thousand troops and forty-six warships deployed in and around Costa Rica. Washington and *San Jose* claim it's to combat the drug trade, but nobody really believes that anymore. Costa Rica is a strategic U.S. military base, plain and simple. Now, while that's true, *San Jose* is touchy about just how true it *looks*."

"Let me guess," I said. "They are furious about the terrorist incident in *Limon* last night and what happened on Highway 32."

"Yes. All activity by the U.S. military is suspended."

"Temporarily..."

"Of course." said Ze'ev. "It will all blow over, but it does affect this mission on several fronts."

"How so," I asked.

"The American embassy disavows any knowledge of our actions. The Navy has not participated in any way, shape or form. The Israeli embassy disavows any prior approvals or assistance. *Mossad* denies any covert presence whatsoever in Costa Rica. Need I go on?"

"No surprises there. I get it. No diplomatic cover, no cavalry or logistics help, no paper trail, no ride home. I'll need a new identity, though. Singleton blew himself up last night."

"Done. Be on the lookout for those birds, but do not engage. Let the bastard get his feet on the ground. I don't want to strike without positive identification... he's so damn elusive. That girl... *Anjela Bravo*... dependable?"

"Yes. By the way, I believe Sabo is in the wooden shed."

"We can get him too, alive, if we do it right."

"They've got lots of boots down there. We don't."

"They are sitting in a bowl. Fish in a barrel."

CHAPTER 25

I hate interviews. I really hate them when my head is cracking, my back is sore, and when I don't remember the sickbay I'm stuck in or how long I've been there.

"Mr. Sheppard… good morning."

"Good Morning. Who are you?"

"I'm Robert Walker, CIA. I'm here to discuss the events surrounding the recent activity in *San Jose*. We are of course aware of your own activities in Costa Rica and Agent Pinsky's recent high interest in the terrorist *Vespula*."

Then it started coming back to me… I was aboard the *USS Freedom*, a littoral combat ship of the United States Navy, Fourth Fleet, SOUTHCOM Operations. I was picked up off a bridge in Costa Rica and transported in a SH-60 Seahawk helicopter, dispatched on my behalf.

The *Freedom* had just completed a seizure of cocaine from smugglers off the northern coast of Columbia. It was a shipment of cocaine with an estimated street value of two hundred and fifty million dollars. That seizure was made possible by information provided by… none other than me. The *Freedom* was also returning from conducting Counter Transnational Organized Crime Operations in the 4th Fleet Area of Responsibility.

"Let me get this straight… I'm under interrogation by the CIA for helping the United States *Navy*? I was assured the Navy would disavow participation… my own included."

"I'm sure they will, as will the CIA. That is standard procedure, and we will be aided with full-throated support from the Costa Rican government. As a former federal agent, Mr. Sheppard, you know how all this works." He sounded slightly impatient.

"And… Ms. Charity Fields," I asked. "And the girl with us?"

"Both heading back to the United States. No questions asked."

"And I'm free to go?"

"Of course, however, the Costa Rican press and an opposition party are screaming bloody murder to our State Department about that gun battle in *San Jose*. The Secretary of State has inquired, too. It doesn't help that an amateur video of that shoot-out went viral. And of course, Costa Rica's Department of Tourism is livid. So, to the best of your ability, I need answers about what happened two days ago…at *El Agujero*… at *The Hole*."

The Hole… the moment Walker said those two words, the details came crashing back into my mind like a runaway Michigan milk truck.

And then I processed his time frame; that hit me even harder.

"Two days!" I was totally shocked. "I've been on this boat for *two days?"*

He nodded, "Yes… sleeping. The women with you left the same day you arrived, but one of them insisted you get fully checked out, nourished and lots of sleep. A certain Israeli agent insisted the same thing. You've had quite an adventure, I'm told."

"It's true. It's a long story."

He nodded again. "I bet it is. But I've got to report everything to my superiors so we can get our cover stories straight. So go for it. I'm all ears."

By midmorning, the day of our rescue attempt, the rain had ceased. Feeling as wet as wind sails, we maintained radio silence and monitored the scene at *The Hole*. It was quiet.

We all knew things were getting complicated when a big armored truck rolled slowly down into *The Hole*, just minutes before the anticipated arrival of *Vespula's* choppers.

Someone had modified a big International CXT pickup truck into an armored personnel carrier by adding a ten foot cargo section in place of the bed, and welding thick steel plates onto the entire truck body. It may as well have been an oblong mini-tank on six wheels. Portals along the sides provided openings for machine gun barrels, and the steel plates rendered the truck impenetrable to most bullets.

It took up space, both in reality and in the minds of conceivable adversaries... people like us. Once it parked, the truck just sat there idling. Its formidable presence did half its work.

"Anybody worried about that?" I asked into our ears, "or is it just me?"

Nobody answered. I didn't blame them. We were about to go hot.

Vespula's choppers came in from the south. Two snipers sat strapped in on the side of each chopper, as Ze'ev foretold. I noted a certain uneasiness in the *Fuerza Publica* cops down below at ground zero... they did not like snipers aiming bolts of lightning down on their heads.

I understood right where they were coming from.

I won't cite needless detail about our own firepower and tactical positioning. We did have three degrees of advantage: the element of surprise, the high ground, and triangular crossfire, and although outnumbered, we were by no means outgunned once those birds landed.

We also had Ze'ev Pinsky, and they did not. We had his military training, his flawless tactics, his precision and his fearless discipline. He brought his deadly KRISS Super V to the party, and another lethal guest... a short-barreled titanium M240L machine gun configured for ground combat.

He was good at that kind of work.

Upon arrival he actually crept up on old Temple, supposedly lying undetectable in thick cover, and softly tapped his shoulder with an

Israeli combat knife. Temple cussed in our collective ears after recovering from cardiac arrest, and we held back our laughter as best we could. Only Ze'ev could pull off something like that. It turned out to be the only light moment of that day.

At the start of things, their numerical advantage counted for little. The upper area surrounding the encampment was bushy and overgrown. Our adversaries would have difficulty detecting us even with the best thermal imaging.

We felt confident we could handle *Vespula's* snipers and spook all the others in the first few crucial moments of engagement. None of us believed that *Aguilera's* ill-prepared *Fuerza Publica* forces would stick around long if harassed by rigorous heavy fire. We were in a good place. We did not want a bloodbath anyway, just a 'clean shoot.'

Chava Cresca had the shot, the most critical assignment of all. We all knew what she could do with that Heckler Koch G36 assault rifle at short distance. *Vespula* would die instantly; that seemed the most likely outcome. Only the armored CXT truck troubled me. We could not see what lay beneath all that plate armor. Something big and bulletproof like that could change the game... and instantly neutralize our triple advantage.

Anjela had the simplest job of all. We did not ask much of her. She simply had to identify *Vespula*, nothing more. To that end, she made a ball out of strangler-vines and kept Spike occupied until those helicopters arrived. It would have been ludicrous to have her hiding in the bushes with a hyperactive dog. But a pretty thing like her might be observed exercising her pooch after a long rain and not raise suspicions. Alas... even a simple objective can sink to fiasco if all outcomes are not foreseen, and that is what happened. What could go wrong did go wrong.

The two helicopters came in, slowly descending. When they did land, *Anjela* inexplicably began walking down a set of long wooden steps toward the heart of *The Hole*— definitely not part of the plan.

"What is she *doing*," I asked, but no one broke cover to stop her.

Too much was at stake.

Vespula's four snipers had already fanned out, on the lookout for threats. The occupants of both choppers disembarked; the spinning blades fanned them with gusts of artificial wind.

I immediately recognized the passengers in the chopper closest to the buildings. Mimi Sabo and *Aguilera* were unmistakable. I also recognized a stout, tough looking woman dressed in a jump suit. She had bright orange hair… my old pal the acid-bath headhunter, the one who marinated Voshe.

Aguilera really knew how to pick them, for sure.

When a man exited the second helicopter, *Anjela* surprised everybody again. We prepped her to provide a simple hand signal, and then to leave *The Hole* and make her way back to the *casabuelo*. Instead, she threw the big vine-ball down the old wooden steps, toward the choppers, and started running *that* way.

Not part of the plan…

Spike sprinted too, chasing the thrown ball. Distracted, a *Vespula* sniper turned. He raised and leveled his scoped rifle, and fired twice. Two chunks of wood blasted up off the wooden steps directly in front of *Anjela*. She almost tumbled trying to stop her forward momentum. She got the sniper's message, though. Spike did not. He ran to the vine-ball and began tearing at it with his little teeth.

The man who left the other chopper raised his hand and appeared to shout, but his words were lost in the whining screams of the choppers' rotary blades. I saw the sniper lower his rifle instantly. The man who ordered him to do so raised his fingers to his lips and whistled. The sound never reached my ears.

Spike looked up, and then suddenly sprinted forward. He ran to the man, who appeared to whistle a second time. Spike leapt up into his arms. I felt convinced we had our man, although *Anjela's* outburst of initiative seemed pointless. She did not have to do all that.

In Ze'ev's world, gunning everybody down would have been just fine… a tad messy, but collateral damage was part of the job. Still, to have *Vespula* identify himself with a show of loving-kindness toward Spike seemed the ultimate final irony.

The only thing left to wait for? The fiery bolt of Israeli justice striking *Vespula* to the muddy ground... I recall wishing that he had worn a flight helmet. I wanted to see another one fly off somebody's head.

But the unthinkable happened again.

Chava Cresca missed the shot.

Her rifle rang out with a singular, muffled 'pop.'

The orange-haired woman's head literally burst, in a 'pink puff' sort of way, and her body fell down flat and dead. A rapid follow-up erupted from Chava's gun, as if she wanted to fix her error, like someone committing a foul in sports after a grievous turnover. But a miss is a miss.

Everybody on both sides reacted. *Vespula* dove to the ground. His men returned sniper shots toward Chava's cover. Ze'ev retaliated. He opened up with the M240L machine gun to suppress the sniper fire and relieve Chava. One of the snipers crumpled, near his boss *Vespula*. The others dove for the sandbags shielding the dwellings. A portal on the steel-plated CXT truck popped open... and a gun-burst ripped into Ze'ev's lair. He answered in kind and I also returned suppression fire. I blew a portal cover off its hinges —pure luck— and then immediately became an earth-lover, ducking the counter-fire unleashed by the steel-plated truck. The whole place lit up then. Several *Fuerza Publica* panicked, shooting wildly into the jungle at phantom targets. *Anjela* sprinted up *The Hole's* wooden stairs. Spike followed. It all happened in a matter of moments. Just like that, a dozen people died... just that quickly.

Aguilera and Mimi Sabo ran and dove for a chopper early on and made it inside, and the AH6 Little Bird began lifting away. *Vespula* tried to do the same but Temple and Ze'ev pinned him down with a barrage of bullets while I kept the steel-plated truck occupied with withering fire. I had my magazines mated together 'jungle style,' (one mag inserted into the gun and the other attached to it, hanging upside down)... when the first one ran out I 'flipped 'em' without losing time, which kept the big steel truck quiet for a few precious seconds...

Vespula made his second run for his chopper, which took innumerable hits from Ze'ev's location, through the fuselage and cockpit. I am certain the pilot got riddled. *Vespula* survived that second salvo and dove full-length back behind the sandbags as his men fired away to provide cover. His wounded AH6 chopper suddenly exploded, and the bird carrying *Aguilera* and Mimi Sabo lowered its nose and began firing a Browning M2 .50 caliber machine gun.

There's a reason the old Browning "Ma Deuce" has served in every conflict since World War I. It kills well... and blasts through substantial chunks of vegetation with ease. All you want to do is hit the dirt.

I saw the tracers hitting Chava Cresca's position. It was ugly. I was scared for her and I hoped Ze'ev would hold his fire and not let the chopper pinpoint his location on the slope. Smartly, we all laid low. We had to, but that allowed *Vespula* to break cover and run to the chopper, followed closely by his gunners, who hopped up on the side benches and fired at random into the brush as they rose away.

Between those shooters and the powerful 'Ma Deuce' they had way too much firepower. In fact, engaging the chopper in the air might have been suicidal. We had also lost the element of surprise; so we had to get out, before the boots below us braved up. But then we took some random small-arms fire too, from behind us... upper perimeter stuff. We always knew they might be there; *Vespula* was a smart enough guy to put eyes on a ridge. We just never had the boots to really spec them out. It was random... no real threat unless they spotted one of us retreating.

I saw a perimeter man moving between our positions, and then ducking and covering in the vegetation. I stayed put, in stealth mode. He drifted down again, more or less in front of me. I raised my weapon and aimed. I could have shot his brains into the next dimension, but I passed.

Instead I swiftly swept in behind him, ninja style, and coldcocked

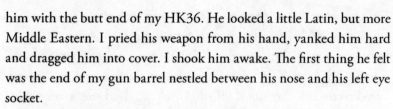

him with the butt end of my HK36. He looked a little Latin, but more Middle Eastern. I pried his weapon from his hand, yanked him hard and dragged him into cover. I shook him awake. The first thing he felt was the end of my gun barrel nestled between his nose and his left eye socket.

"Tell me one time, 'No speak English'... and it'll be the last thing you ever tell anybody. Where are you from?"

"I speak it. I speak the English. I am from *Karaj*... Alborz Province... Iran." He said it like it was a death sentence, not a good thing. He wanted to live.

"Where is Sabo?"

"I don't know Sabo."

Bam! I punched his face. "Wrong answer asshole! Where is Sabo?"

"They no tell me Sabo!"

Bam! Bam! "Sabo!" He knew something...

"They will kill my family if I say Sabo... *please!*"

"Then I will kill them too... worse!" I pushed the gun barrel firmly between his eyes. "*Yar.hamu-ka-Llâh,*" I said coldly, which meant, 'may Allah have mercy on your soul'.

"*He is in the shed down there!* I never see him much. They never tell me everything. I know he is there. *Vespula*... he come today to take him. Sabo not know, but... his own daughter put him there."

"Tell me why... tell me why and I swear I will let you live."

"How I know you not lying to me..."

"You don't..." I nudged the barrel just a little. "Trust me..."

"Sabo... he have a chip... information."

"A chip with money on it," I said. "*Vespula's* money..."

The Iranian shook his head. "He no care about money! He care about chip. Chip have money, yes... have password... yes. Chip have *names* too... *many names*... my name... all names."

I could hear the chopper fading in retreat, voices below us shouting, the sound of the big armored truck's wheels whining, and its engine roaring as if mired in the mud. The massive truck was too heavy for the current terrain conditions... I remembered my early Wing Chung training... *Even the greatest strength can be a weakness if properly exploited.*

"Whose names? Whose names are on the chip?"

"Gamaat Islamiya in Egypt, Lashkar-e-Taiba in Pakistan, Hezbollah, Hamas, Palestinian Islamic Jihad... many more... FARC, the cartels... all bad people. Me, I am on it too... but I am not like them. I am a good person."

"Those aren't people, nice guy," I said. "Those are organizations. There is nothing secret about them!" *Bam!* I straight jabbed him in the chest as hard as I could. I guess I was frustrated. "You tryin' to play me? I ought to blow your brains out..."

"No!" He coughed up blood. That caught me off guard. I did hit him hard, but it was only a straight jab. "Please," he pleaded, "I am sick. I got the chest cancer. I only wish to go home to *Karaj.*"

"Nobody cares. If you want to go home alive, talk."

"Okay, I talk. When USA kill Osama bin Laden, take all computers. They say, 'we find things'... but they not find all things... Osama have three wives..."

"Lucky guy. So what?"

"All wives deported by Pakistan to Saudi Arabia... youngest wife... Amal? She have chip in Saudi Arabia... inside her... give to man from Palestine, a *Hamas* man. The *Hamas* man gives chip to *Vespula*. Chip have Osama bin Laden plan and many names. Big bank boss steal money and chip from *Vespula*. Sabo number two bank boss... steal chip from big boss... Sabo not know names on chip."

"How do you know all this?"

"My job... make Sabo talk."

"So you lied to me... you do know Sabo. You torture people."

"Yes... like you. I good man though... like you, yes? You let me go then... Sabo in wood shed...others too."

"What others?"

The man coughed. "*Kidon.*"

I rewarded his candor with life. But I coldcocked him again.

The few *Fuerza Publica* remaining had begun a hasty retreat, as *Vespula, Aguilera* and Mimi Sabo swooped off to freedom. That left only the armored truck and the frightened stragglers shooting potshots at defenseless palm trees.

Chava Cresca had strangely gone silent... no response to our 'chirps and whistles'... and for a fighter like her, it meant we had every right to think the worst. To be honest, I was angry as hell.

For whatever reason, call it 'Mission Tunnel' if you fancy, I ultimately decided to nab Sabo out from the wooden structure. Ze'ev had just told us to pull out. I 'rogered' and Temple 'rogered' but, once more, Chava did not. I told Ze'ev I had to go check on her. He opposed. Tactically speaking, Ze'ev was correct; the circumstances dictated our quick exit.

Well, I guess Ze'ev would not be himself without exercising ruthless tactical discipline, but I wouldn't be myself without trying to save someone who had helped me in a crunch. We argued until he submitted; he said he would go check himself.

It was during that heated discussion that I saw a Resplendent *Quetzal* flying across the length of *The Hole*. Mind you, we were still in a combat situation, albeit a hasty retreat mode.

I suppose that every bird in the vicinity had vacated when the shooting started. Seeing the legendary bird flying across *The Hole* struck me as odd. It flew calmly across the carnage, landing atop the wooden structure. No, I am not cracked in the head... not glamorizing the incident... that is truly where it landed. I could not believe it either. I raised a pair of small binoculars to pull it in closer... and incredibly, the *Quetzal* had only one long tail feather... that's right... just one.

I stared long and hard. I felt that strange feeling I had back on the roof of the *casabuelo*, the sensation that an old spirit wanted my attention. My eyes scanned the dead lying on the ground. I heard sirens moaning in the distance... but not yet getting closer... the cops usually avoided *Los Guido,* surely now they would come.

I scanned the dead again...contemplating...

I believe each dead body has a spirit life... maybe the shells lay empty, but something lives on. I took one more look at the *Quetzal.* It had begun grooming itself, and then it stopped. It looked directly at me before departing its perch and flying off to find a more peaceful habitation.

The moment it lifted off, I whispered to the spirit of my ancestor, *"If Sabo lives, then send the bird back to me..."*

In what amounted to an astonishing event in my life, the *Quetzal* suddenly changed course, executing a sweeping arc that exposed its back and its long outstretched wings to the now-shining sun. As if summoned, it returned. It flew past the wooden structure and settled on the highest branch of a nearby tree, too close to be mere coincidence. It stared at me momentarily, and then flew away again.

"Phillip," said Ze'ev's voice in my earphone... "I'm sorry. I located her position...she is not here. I found some gear, and some blood... not a lot but some... but not her... I think she may have been hit... tried to get away... She may be trekking back to the *casabuelo*... or she may be... in deep trouble."

But I had stopped listening. In my mind she was gone, Ze'ev not there, Temple irrelevant... whether or not *Anjela* had made it to safety with Spike completely beside the point.

"Ze'ev," I said, "at my site you will find an Iranian man... he may provide intel on *Vespula*'s next move... He may also provide intel on the terrorist names on the Sabo chip... He told me about those names, even if you did not. I can't help but wonder why."

There was only silence, and in that silence I began moving toward the wooden structure. At the same time, I heard the steel-plated CXT truck free itself from the mud and go on the move. I knew the truck would also advance to Sabo's location.

I pulled my earphone from my ear. It dropped uselessly at my feet.

No one could help me do what I had to do... I saw the Resplendent *Quetzal* in my mind, its red breast, bright as blood... I heard the old voice, that of my ancestor, speaking...

With the assault rifle slung on my back, I ran toward the wooden structure, eyeing the two openings that served as windows, shuttered with canvas. I pulled a flash-bang grenade from a leg packet, yanked the ring and with my fist punched through the canvas and dropped the grenade just inside the window. I pulled another from my opposite pocket and stuffed that one through the second shuttered window. They ignited consecutively.

I bolted around the structure, to the front, and as I rounded the last corner I saw the front end of the CXT truck. I dove back behind the corner of the building as someone fired from a front opening. The salvo ripped right through the corner of the building like it was cardboard.

The shooter kept blazing bullets through that particular corner, perhaps in the hope that I was stupid enough to believe that ducking around a corner would provide safe haven from a high-powered gun.

Well, I am no fool, which is why I survived that barrage.

Still, I had no choice but to enter the building, especially to capitalize on the flash-bang grenade effects. So, I took three quick steps back and charged the outside wall with all my might, literally throwing myself at it like a madman.

I went crashing through. The entire building was smoke-filled, the best light source being the wall planks I had just knocked down. I saw someone dragging a body out the front door.

I moved toward that man, and through the haze I saw a rifle barrel poking out in front of me. I deflected the barrel to the side, just before it fired, and punched the body holding it. We were suddenly engaged in a life and death struggle for the rifle. We fought blindly. His hands tried to strike me and control the weapon, as we swung, kicked, twisted and grappled each other. I knew if he broke free with the gun I was a dead man, and he knew the same.

He tried holding his portion of the rifle and at the same time jumping on top of me. I braced my legs and swung one elbow up and into his body again and again until I got lucky and broke through to his chin. He grunted and lost his grip on the rifle at the same time I did, and it dropped to the floor. We each grabbed the other, to prevent either one of us from reaching the gun. He also tried wrenching the HK36 from my back. In response, I made every effort to rip his throat out. He screamed and tried to thumb-gouge my eye, but it ended up in my mouth and I bit down on it mercilessly…and began punching his groin viciously as well— it was that kind of death fight. We tumbled to the floor, punching, kicking, kneeing… essentially fighting for the right to live. We thrashed and struggled like wolves, and suddenly with a snaking twist he broke free, kicked me away with both legs fully extended and then lunged for the rifle.

Just as he reached for it, a phantom foot kicked it away. He scrambled for it again as I brought the HK36 off my back, slung it around, and pointed forward. I saw him take hold of his own gun, control it, bring it around, and point it where I lay. I rolled desperately to one side and onto my back with my head pointed toward him. He fired, sitting up. I fired from my back, shooting across my own forehead with my eyes looking 'up' toward him sitting on the floor. His shots drilled the floor space I had momentarily occupied… my shots struck home and ended the matter emphatically.

I rolled to my feet, looking about, holding the HK36, ready to shoot anything that moved. I saw three men in the haze, all tied to chairs, all in various states of injurious torture. Each was blindfolded and strapped in, but one man had managed to free a leg. He had just saved my life.

I heard the CXT truck's throaty growl. It began to drive off… I had seen a body being dragged away, but rather than pursue, first I ran to the men strapped in their chairs. I helped to untie the one who had saved me.

"Who are you," I asked.

"Singer, Interpol," he said.

"Cut the bull. *Kidon* or *Mossad*," I said.

"*Kidon*, all of us," he confessed. "Somebody burned us."

I'm here with Pinsky," I said. "Where is Sabo?"

"They took him just now. Hired cartel gunmen. Go after them. I will free the others."

I stepped to the dead man and yanked the machine gun from his useless hands. I shoved it at the man called Singer. "Get out of here if you can."

"We will. Stop *them!*" cried Singer.

I didn't dare go out the front, so I left the same way I came in. It made perfect sense. Outside, I heard the CXT truck whining in the mud again. I circled around panther-like, cautiously passing the 'Swiss cheese' corner where I had first engaged the CXT. I saw the back wheels of the plated truck spinning in vain. The weight of all that steel had twice betrayed the occupants. A man was kneeling beside one wheel, forcing a wooden plank beneath it, hoping to regain traction to free the truck from the mire. He saw me, and reached for his waistline. I pointed the HK36 at him and pulled the trigger, but my weapon unaccountably jammed.

The man raised his gun, but before he fired I hurled my HK36 at him, striking his shoulder as he fired. He missed. I sprinted back the way I came as he leapt up and followed, determined to end it. I tumbled. He caught up to me, and without a word pointed a semiautomatic pistol at me. We both heard loud crashings and the sound of an engine roaring through the thick green brush, and suddenly, with a tremendous roar, the *Pinzgauer* crashed free from the jungle.

It barreled in and struck the shooter. He sailed like a wind-tossed rag, right through the outside wall and into the building. A machine gun inside 'ripped a burst' as the *Pinz* rumbled into reverse.

Charity was sitting in the right-hand passenger seat. "Sorry about that wall," she said. I ignored her and jumped inside. The big steel CXT had freed itself. It started forcing its way up the long slope of *The Hole*, laboring to the top.

"Get after that truck!' I shouted.

"Si!"

When I looked at the driver, It was *Anjela Bravo.*

"Oh no, not you," I said, angrily. "You don't follow orders!"

"I sorry I mess up! But I still fight for you!"

"Just go," I yelled, pointing to the CXT clambering up the slope. "Get a move on! Sabo is in that truck."

We gave chase. The CXT reached the upper ridge and gained traction on a wet, dirt road while the *Pinz's* all-terrain drive pushed us to the top despite the thickness of the brush. Soon enough, we hit the dirt road too. The *Pinz* roared after the CXT as the heavier vehicle gouged its way along the rain-soaked road.

"Where are they going," asked Charity, as the *Pinz* threw us about roughly. *Anjela* seemed to go only top speed, and possessed an annoying knack for finding every bump in the road.

"I don't know, but that truck has got Sabo inside," I said, "and his money chip is also loaded with the goods on every terrorist worth clocking. Osama bin Laden once owned the chip, so every government in the free world wants a look-see." I then asked Charity, "Hey, how did you find us?"

"I didn't" she said "Ze'ev tracked *us* down with this." My watch jangled loosely on her wrist. "We found the *Pinz* much the same way."

"Where is T'zvi," I asked.

"Behind you," said Charity.

I looked back in the cargo area. T'zvi wore a set of headphones and had plugged into the *Pinz's* radio. "Good to be back aboard," he said. "I hope I don't get in your way."

"Can you raise Ze'ev? Or Temple... are they okay?"

"They are fine," said T'zvi. "Temple has headed north to a small town off the *Costanera* Highway, called *Capulln,* just past the *Tárcoles* River... there is a patch of land suitable there and Temple will arrange air transport for you back to the United States. By the way, that big truck is using a standard radio. I'm picking up their signal. Sabo owns a secret home in a rich beach town to the West... *Jaco.* I am not certain, but they may be headed there. Are you familiar?"

"Very," I said testily. "I need weapons. What have we got."

"Well I cannot tell you for sure, because of my limitations," said T'zvi, "but there seems to be two assault rifles, and plenty of ammo, and the dazzler rifles, too. Oh, and I feel at least a dozen XMU 300's, the powerful flash bang grenades."

"Good," I said. "Pass an assault rifle up here, and the ammo, and half a dozen flash-bangs." I hung some flash-bangs on my waist and stuffed others in my cargo pockets. "I don't know what we are looking at, but I don't want to wish I had something I need."

"What can *we* do?" asked Charity

"Help me stop that truck. Sabo is inside. I want his information now more than ever. If *Anjela* can get me close I think I can disable it or force them to stop."

The CXT truck speeded on ahead now, all nine tons of it. It rumbled down the road like a charging rhino, constantly sinking in the mud but pushing through by the awesome power of its 500 cubic inch engine. Our lighter *Pinzgauer* offered up speed and agile power, with no weight issues, and *Anjela* now seemed to understand the need for us to avoid the bigger truck's pitfalls.

"Damn that steel truck is big," said Charity.

She was right. The CXT dwarfed the *Pinz*, which weighed in at only four tons. We could not muscle them off the road. We could not outgun them either.

Still, I felt if we could flank the truck, and I could mount it, then I could exploit its greatest weakness: the same armor that protected those inside would prevent them from shooting me while I operated right on top of them. I envisioned a saber-toothed cat leaping onto the back of a woolly mammoth stranded in a tar pit.

We caught them in short order. I told *Anjela* to stay well back and be prepared to swerve off if the CXT began firing from the rear. They eventually bogged down in a rain-induced mud flat on the road.

We were traveling too fast.

"Stop *Anjela*!" I shouted. She slammed on the brakes and the *Pinz* began a long straight slide that sent mud and water flying high on either side, until we stopped. Seizing the opportunity, I leapt from the *Pinz* and sprinted for the CXT.

I had to cover twenty yards before the CXT shifted low and worked itself loose from its muddy "tar pit." Heaven knows I've lost a step over the years, but I covered the ground well and jumped up on the back end just as the truck began pulling away. I clambered quickly to the top to minimize my vulnerability, and felt gratified to find several conveniently placed hand holds, which apparently had been included in the design. I felt relatively safe despite the wet conditions that still existed on the road. I seriously doubted they would risk trying to shoot me through their own armor.

The CXT broke mud and hit the pavement.

Toting the HK36, I edged to the side of the truck with the open portal, the one I had shot open earlier, at *The Hole*. I pulled a XM100 from my belt and calmly tossed it inside. I shortly heard its strong blast. Thick smoke began billowing from inside. I then worked my way to the other side and took aim at another portal. I blasted away the hinges with two short bursts of gunfire. The portal cover fell off and bounced upon the road behind us. Just as quickly, I tossed in another XM100, and was rewarded with another powerful blast.

Someone in the cargo area did not like my generosity. They stuck their arm through an open portal, the one I had just damaged, and brandished an SR-15 submachine gun. Standard bad-guy issue, I thought, as I scrambled to get off the top. I hung my body over the side of the truck to avoid any gunfire and flinched when the SR15 sprayed the top of the truck blindly. I just happened to be hanging on the side in such a way that my chest blocked another closed portal and prevented anyone from taking action from there. Every time they pushed I used my upper body to force it closed. This mini-drama played out as the truck picked up speed and regained its equilibrium on the road.

I abandoned my grip with one hand, fumbled and grappled, desperately trying to grab hold of another flash bang grenade and also keep the blocked portal closed at the same time. Finally I felt confident in my grip, and shifted my body slightly to the side. The portal cover flew open and banged against the steel plating, and just as quickly I tossed the stun grenade inside.

"Thank you," I said, to whoever pushed the portal open. I banged victoriously on the cover to anger the occupants. One of them pushed the portal open again and stuck out his SR15 machine gun. I grabbed his wrist, and when the gun began firing, I forced the barrel to point at the ground so that all the shots flew off the mark. I also tossed in another stunner grenade.

It blew, and the submachine gun went silent.

I tossed in another birthday surprise, and suddenly the truck began lurching at full speed. I looked back. *Anjela* was still in pursuit and approaching us from behind. A gunman tried one more time to spray me from a portal but I was ready; I pinned the gun and his forearm against the steel plating. The truck hit a bump and I bounced and landed flat on my stomach, but I never let go of his wrist, and his hand never let go of the SR15. So I got ugly and bit his wrist, like an animal. That's one way to disarm somebody.

Then I tossed in my last two stun grenades for good measure.

But the driver would not concede. With smoke billowing from the CXT, we barreled down the road as fast as the engine would take us, with the *Pinz* in hot pursuit. I looked back at my colleagues. They must have thought me insane. I admit I had one singular focus… stop that truck and get Sabo.

However, the odds for success plummeted once I saw an AH6 helicopter flying in at an attack angle behind the pursuing *Pinz*. I knew immediately that the chopper was *Vespula's* getaway bird.

I waved signals to try and warn them, but my frantic efforts came too late. I watched helplessly as the chopper opened fire with its ferocious 'Ma Deuce' .50 caliber gun, shooting for the rear of the *Pinz*.

Chunks of road behind them began popping up, and only at the last moment did the *Pinz* swerve to avoid being blown to bits— and that is *exactly* what would have happened if the .50 caliber had landed home, make no mistake about that.

I thought the *Pinz* would tip over, but I never saw it recover, because in that same instant I realized that the chopper was firing at me too, at the end of its attack run. I scrambled and hung from the left side, just as a short barrage of .50 caliber bullets blasted straight down through top of the CXT. No random ricochets occurred, like you might see in the movies; those .50 caliber bullets cut through that armor like it was not even there.

That's when I knew I was in deep trouble.

The CXT truck driver saw me clinging in his side view mirror, while straight ahead, two extra wide-load trucks approached in the opposite direction, hauling pre-fab houses. Those babies were *wide*, and I knew I better pull myself to the top of the truck, and I tried, but I failed, because my arms and hands were fatigued. I tried once more as the trucks grew closer, only to fail again.

The CXT driver observed this in his side mirror, and I knew what he was thinking before he even executed his move... he started drifting ever so gently into the opposing lane, hoping to sideswipe me into oblivion. I was not about to go out like *that*. With whatever energy I had left, I started working my way down the side of the truck, toward the rear.

The first truck sounded its horn but failed to avoid the CXT, and knocked the side-view mirror off when it scraped the steel-plated pickup along the side. Sparks flew and I swung to the rear just in time to feel a roaring blur blow by me, and then another, inches from my left shoulder. If I had stayed put I would have been hamburger meat. I looked back after the trucks raced by, and saw the *Pinz* drift far right, to avoid the trouble. One truck driver blew his horn loud, hard and long, like a passing train.

By then *Vespula*'s chopper had returned for another blasting run.

This time it ignored the *Pinz*, intent upon making another run at me. Obviously, *Vespula* and *Aguilera* both had it in for me, and I needed no further convincing that Sabo was inside the CXT. Whatever Sabo had on them, they did not want me knowing.

Their snipers began taking shots from the right side, so I had no choice… I shifted back to the driver's side of the CXT and hung on tight. Their bullets bounced off the steel plates like pebbles off a tool shed. The chopper maneuvered for a better angle and two shots barely missed as I shifted back to the rear, playing a deadly game of cat and mouse. By then I was not reacting with lightning-quick reflexes, but as the chopper came around again, a long gun barrel emerged from the passenger side of the *Pinz*. A huge, canon-like blast sounded, and then seconds later another. It had to be Charity, shooting the shotgun, and I guessed she was firing the Thor's Thunder rounds. They could do nothing but make noise at that distance, but they drew the chopper's attention away from me, and the snipers fired potshots at the *Pinz* as it swerved and careened to thwart their efforts.

As I hung to the side of the truck by one hand, I felt a tremendous fear for Charity, T'zvi and *Anjela*, more so than I felt for myself. I could not just hang there and watch them get shot at, so with my free hand I pulled my HK36 rifle off my back, swung it around, laid it over the top of the CXT and fired on the chopper. I had next-to-nil chances of hitting it as we flew down the highway, but that was beside the point. I kept thinking about Chava, the fire she took from the snipers as she hunkered down in *The Hole,* and I kept hearing Ze'ev's voice… *I think she may have been hit… I think she may have been hit… I think she may have been hit…*

I just wanted to draw fire away from my girls. I succeeded, perhaps more than I fully intended. The snipers took more shots at me instead, and a quick burst of fire from the .50 caliber blasted through the truck again. I heard the bullets slam into the ground beneath us, having ripped straight through with brutal indifference. Something in the undercarriage buckled, but the truck rolled on. Another .50 caliber blast cut through the plating at an angle and I suddenly heard and felt thudding *pings* as bullet fragments bounced around the inside of the CXT's steel shell. I knew those ricochets could kill instantly, especially anybody standing.

I hoped it wasn't Sabo… but I was glad it wasn't me.

My HK36's clip was empty and I had no more ammo, so I tossed the gun behind my back again. None of the CXT's side portals had opened for some time. I was sure the occupants had taken hits when the .50 caliber bullets bounced around the inside of their mobile fortress.

I also realized it was only a matter of time before the chopper made another run at me. With no side mirror, the driver could not see down his flank anymore, where I hung precariously at the end of my tether. Creeping forward and commandeering the truck seemed iffy, if not completely outlandish, but I felt out of options; that chopper had drastically changed everything. I was losing badly, and sometimes it works to chuck caution aside… but not usually.

I looked back one more time. I could see the loyal *Pinz* plugging along. I waved them off. I wanted them to pull back, to stop pursuing. I didn't want them getting shot at any more. Instead, the *Pinz* sped up and tried getting closer.

"Damn you, *Anjela*…" I muttered. She never did exactly as she was told, and then there was the issue of Chava…if *Anjela* had not exceeded her role at *The Hole*, Chava might have made that shot.

I think she may have been hit… I think she may have been hit…

I waved *Anjela* off again, more fiercely, but she steadfastly refused to obey, using the *Pinz's* lighter weight and quicker acceleration to maintain pursuit. I cursed her under my breath.

It was then that I saw the chopper far away, shadowing the *Pinz*. It had circled around and gone high, but it would angle down sharply for its last deadly kill-run. I was out of ammo, out of energy, and just clinging for life. I had abandoned the foolish notion of making a run at the driver. Suddenly, the *Pinz* zoomed in alongside the CXT. Charity leaned out of the passenger window with the most desperate look I had

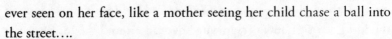

ever seen on her face, like a mother seeing her child chase a ball into the street....

"Jump on!" she screamed. She actually expected me to do that?

I shook my head no.

"You can do it!"

Yeah, she actually expected me to try. Moreover, she *believed* I could pull it off. Flattering, but I knew otherwise. She had watched lots of action movies, I suppose.

"*Get the hell outta here!*" I yelled. Even if I could have accomplished such a movie stunt, it would only serve to put them in more peril. I knew that *Vespula* and *Aguilera* would stop at nothing to kill me now—and anyone with me. I knew the mentality of men like them... I was a thorn in their sides and they would make me pay dearly.

My eyes locked onto Charity's and I screamed one more time, *"Get outta here!"*

"No! You can do it," she screamed. "I know you can do it!"

But I knew it was hopeless, and I knew it was foolish to try. I looked at her grimly and shook my head. Her eyes said plenty, and I thought they might be the last beautiful things I saw in this world. Then the CXT truck driver looked back over his shoulder and veered hard left, forcing *Anjela* to swerve and back off. That settled things. The CXT had forcefully ended our fierce, tender subplot. So much for love and glory, right? You might think so, but don't count on it; Charity is tough and stubborn as hell.

The chopper made its move. The bastards were swooping in fast and low, extraordinarily low. And I knew why... it was personal. It was calculated ruthlessness. They had decided to pull the old Darth Vader *'I have you now'* clearing run. They would shoot the *Pinz* 'straight up the ass' with the big gun, and let the snipers pick me off as they zoomed on by. Just because they could? Yeah, why not?

I frantically waved off the *Pinz*, but once again headstrong *Anjela* zoomed in behind the CXT and hung close, refusing to give up her ineffectual chase, as if she could somehow save me. The CXT would not allow itself to be flanked again and would knock the *Pinz* clear off the road if it tried. With its weight advantage, that would be simple enough.

The chopper's big gun opened up on the *Pinz* just as I had foreseen… However, to my utter surprise, in response the *Pinz's* driver-side rear door swung open. A thick black barrel emerged, rather like a telescope, and pointed toward the chopper. I heard no shot, saw no flash, observed no tracer fire, but the chopper suddenly lurched, and turned abruptly. Its tail dropped and then recovered, but the pilot overcompensated. Its nose then pointed down too quickly, and the pilot overcorrected again, much too hurriedly.

The AH6 was in trouble.

Then the thick, black barrel behind *Anjela* withdrew, and in its place another, smaller rifle emerged. A sharp, crisp barrage of tracer fire ripped from the *Pinz* and bullets slammed into chopper's fuselage as it frantically tried to right itself. Another surprise burst sounded, and bright sparks flew from the chopper's tail section.

Death spiral! It happened that quickly.

As the trucks barreled down the road, the ACH6 spun madly and then rolled like a listless, dying whale. Propellers flailing, it roared and crashed ingloriously to the ground.

The impact looked horrendous, but it did not explode immediately.

Further away now, as I still hung from the side of the big CXT, I saw a single figure scurrying crab-like from the wreckage. It crawled, then scampered, and finally ran… approximating the ascent of Man from tiny primate, to brutish ape, to upright human. As the running man reached the road's shoulder, the chopper exploded with delayed fury, erupting into an orange fireball. The sound reached me shortly after the flash, as a pillar of black smoke sent a death signal to the sky. The escaping man fell forward, then rose and scrambled away. Amazed, I stared at the carnage as it faded in the distance.

Then I looked forward and saw the speeding train.

Yeah, sometimes you go from one mess to another.

It was off to our right, and close enough to cause me real concern, and when the CXT truck accelerated, I got scared. They were going to try to beat the train to a railroad crossing… great.

Trust me, I wanted no part of that action. So once again, I moved to the back of the plated truck. If it sounds like I had a plan, don't kid yourself. There is nothing in the Specialist handbook about beating trains to railroad crossings while you cling to the back of a truck. I will say this… jumping off is not an attractive choice either, no matter how fit you think you are. I was prepared to jump, though. I took one last look back and saw that *Anjela* had stopped… finally she had showed some sense.

I was a goner though…

I can't tell you the braking specs of an eight ton vehicle like the steel-plated CXT. I do know that at the last possible moment, the driver chickened out and slammed on the brakes. I also know I got pinned to the back of the truck from the sudden deceleration. I could not have jumped off even if I wanted to. And I know when I opened my eyes I saw no bed of virgins, no army of angels and no pearly gates. I heard no sweet choir. I only saw the back of the truck and heard the steady clacking sound of a train rolling on its track. I also heard and felt a continuous scraping sound toward the front of the truck. It was only when I pulled myself to the top of the truck and moved to the front that I realized the truck's nose was scraping against train boxcars periodically… not enough to pull the truck onto the tracks… just enough to make that scraping sound. When the bewildered driver stepped out of the CXT, I jumped down behind him. I secured my empty HK36, shoved his shoulder and pointed the barrel at his chest when he turned around. He simply held up his keys and said, "I just drive the truck, *Señor*… I want no trouble."

"Me either," I said, and slammed the butt of my HK36 into his right chin. He struck the ground and went to sleep. I sang no lullabies.

When the *Pinz* rolled up, Charity, *Anjela* and T'zvi came out to greet me.

"Game is not over people," I said, as I checked the unconscious driver for weapons. "Watch those portals. We've got to open up this baby and see what's inside. I know somebody's in there, but I don't know if they are still alive. The chopper shot through to the inside, and those bullets could have bounced around and killed everybody. Exercise extreme caution. They could be just waiting for us…"

They were waiting, all right… for a decent burial. Six men lay shot dead inside the armored cargo section. Once those .50 caliber bullets passed through like lead demons, and fragments bounced off the inside walls, everybody got torn to pieces… it was ugly, to say the least… and once again the axiom passed through my mind… *Even the greatest strength can be a weakness, if properly exploited.*

We heard a man's voice whimpering among the bloody corpses. We sought him out. I never would have guessed…

"Sabo?"

I barely recognized him from mission photos and a related newspaper clipping. He looked like he had caught smallpox on Sunday and bugged a beehive on Monday.

"Conga ants?" I asked. He nodded miserably. "I thought I got it bad, but I see what happens if they're left untreated. You're safe now, Sabo. Anything broke… No? You sure? Good… You speak good English? Good… Your wife sent me to save you. Mission accomplished, so far. I want to get you home… no press, no reporters, all that mess, because your story's not worth the ink needed to put it to print. I want you to know that I'd just as soon drop you off where we found you if you try playing amnesia about that chip. By now you know it's about more than the money. So where is it, Sabo?"

"I lost it…"

"Yeah, right. Here we go…" I was about to help him find it with my right fist, but just before I swung, another *Quetzal* bird landed on top of the open cargo door of the CXT truck.

Not the same one... it had a broader chest and two good tail feathers... it also had a different look in its eyes, like that of a hawk... or a Specialist. Charity and *Anjela* saw it too. It made a chirping sound and began snapping its graceful tail feathers rhythmically like a long whip. Angela spoke, and then whispered something to the bird, and I asked Charity to translate.

"She said there's a Guatemalan legend about the Spaniards... the conquistadors. They crossed the ocean looking for gold... there was a long battle between them and the *Quiches*, a tribe. The *Quiches* lost. Afterwards, *Quetzal* birds flew onto the battlefield. They landed on the *Quiches'* bodies and *Quiche* blood stained their chests. That's why *Quetzals* have bright red breasts."

"Wow... but what did she whisper to the bird."

"She told the bird to watch over you... to help you keep your secrets... because your heart is good."

The train had passed by then, and it was quiet. When the bird flew away, we heard the sound of sirens. I told the others to get back to the *Pinz* and bring it up immediately.

After they left, I turned to Sabo. "Lost my ass... where did you hide the chip? I know *Aguilera's* cops searched your *San Jose* home and probably some people for *Vespula, too*. So where is it, Sabo?"

"I have a secret home in *Jaco*. There is a flat screen television in my wife's study. It is older. They made a slot for an SD chip in the front. I put the chip in that slot. I covered the slot carefully with a logo so you cannot see it anymore."

"Fine, finally we are getting somewhere. So why trust me?"

"I don't trust anyone. But my grandmother immigrated to Costa Rica from Guatemala. She was *Quiche*. She spoke the old tongue. She told *me* that story. That girl there, the pretty, young one... her *Quiche* blood runs strong. She has the power to talk to animals..."

"Come on..."

"It's true. Animals do not fear her and they speak to her. The green bird was speaking when it waved its tail over and over. That is the sign among my grandmother's people. So when she said what she said, I knew I could tell you and no harm would come to me."

"Well keep your secrets to yourself from here on out... and let me ask you something..." The *Pinz* drove up and stopped. "Why did you do it? Why throw a good life away?"

"For riches, men will do stupid things, and evil things... just like the *Conquistadores*... you see?"

I nodded. "Yeah, I see."

CHAPTER 26

We headed west and returned to *Jaco*, the same coastal town where *Aguilera's* men had dismembered Voshe and very nearly me as well. I had come full circle. Life is funny that way.

The Sabo home sat high and mighty on a steep grassy slope, facing the Pacific Ocean in the *Chalets Alta Vista* area of *Jaco*. It looked good enough to be a diplomat's retreat, or a corrupt banker's hideaway. You could walk to the beach in minutes or see the world from a spacious deck that overlooked a precipitous drop of about sixty feet down to a swimming pool and a guesthouse.

I told *Anjela* and T'zvi to wait outside on the road. *Anjela* acted strange, like she didn't want to sit in the *Pinz* anymore. I chalked it up to her headstrong ways, so I made it very clear I wanted her to stay put. She didn't say anything. T'zvi acted strangely too. I concluded that like me, everybody felt exhausted and worn out. When it was all over, we would go back to being our normal selves.

Charity and I took Sabo to the showy front entrance.

"Charity, I am still trying figure out how you took down the chopper... who taught you to shoot?"

"My husband. Well, my dead ex-husband, a long time ago. He was a skeet shooter as a kid, a champ. I know my way around a gun."

"I never knew that..."

"You never asked. You assume. There's a lot about me you don't know. You should take the time..."

I tried in vain to contact Mrs. Sabo on her cell phone. It would have been my first contact since the hotel in Santa Monica. Oddly enough, her mailbox was full. I had not told Sabo of Mimi's fate in the helicopter... I did not want to spoil his homecoming; it also might have tainted his newfound contriteness.

Inside, lots of natural light filtered in softly. Everything had a luxury finish to it. A 'fancy show of one's means of life' would best describe the place. I had a strange sensation that someone was watching us, but Sabo seemed quite relieved to be there. He spoke very highly of his wife, and seemed to regret putting her through hard times. He acted relaxed, as though he would never have to face prosecution or fear for his life ever again.

I let him cling to his delusions.

His mood changed drastically, however, when we entered his wife's study. We came upon her seated in a comfortable, burgundy leather chair. A black cherry electronic cigarette dangled from the corner of her once-luscious lips and her eyes stared blankly across the room to some meaningless spot on the floor. She was dead. Sabo collapsed when he saw her.

"Oh dear Lord, forgive me!" he cried. "Look what they did to her... look what they did to her!" He sobbed openly and kept repeating that same phrase over and over. It seemed the moment he saw her lifeless body, he was a broken man. Charity and I gave him his space. I was tempted to search the flat screen television for the all-important data chip, but I held off. Something told me to wait.

I let him cry it out for quite a while.

I figured he had that coming, but after a time I said, "Sabo, your wife hired me to bring you out and get you back here alive. I did that. I feel for you... but there is the issue of my compensation...and of course the chip." Charity gave me the harshest look I ever saw delivered to anyone. She could do that so well.

Yeah, I know I sounded crass and callous, but in the end I work for pay, not for platitudes. Plus, it did not take a rocket scientist to realize that if I did not get my money that day, I would never see it at all. I simply ignored Charity's judgmental expressions.

Sabo pointed to a large portrait hanging on the wall.

Ah, yes... the secret wall safe behind the prized work of art... how often life imitates fiction, I thought. The portrait swung open on tiny hinges, like a barn door. The wall safe was an old *Hercules* from the 1950's, made by a company called Meilink. It seemed out of place in a modern home, and someone had recently tampered with its mechanisms. "Sabo... this safe is archaic," I said, manipulating the black dial. "I've cracked this model many times. It was made to be fireproof, not burglar-proof. If you installed it as a collectible, fine and dandy, but I would never put anything of real value in it again." I turned to look at him. "The numbers, if you please?"

He nodded and thought a while, sadness still distorting his face, and finally provided the combination.

Sometimes it's tough not to succumb to greed. I found two hundred thousand dollars American, fresh, and a *SIG Sauer* compact 9mm handgun hidden behind the stack of bills.

I only took my twenty-five thousand dollar cut. I left the gun hidden where it lay. I closed the *Hercules* safe and handed the cash over to Charity. She shook her head in dismay, still bothered by my lack of sympathy— but she still took it.

"At least I'm not greedy," I said dryly. "Besides, I don't need the bad karma. Try not to lose it, Charity. Some of it goes to you."

I explained to Sabo how and why I took the case. I asked him if he ever considered that his own daughter might have been involved in trying to find out the location of the chip, at his expense.

Sabo sobbed. "No, no, Mimi would never betray me. They kidnapped her too... they told me so. They threatened to torture her if I refused to give up the chip. I swore to tell them everything if they let her go. I only asked to see her alive."

Boy, did she have him fooled. She would never deceive him again.

I turned to cover the safe. My right hand had barely touched the barn-door picture frame when a voice behind me said, "Thank you for all your hard work, Phillip."

I turned around. T'zvi Pinsky stood across the room in the doorway. He had ditched the blind man's cane in favor of a semiautomatic pistol. Only his prosthetic right hand distinguished him from his valiant twin brother Ze'ev.

"What's this all about T'zvi?" I asked, after a short pause. "I thought we were all on the same team…"

Had he played everyone all these years?

I must admit the notion momentarily shocked me… then I remembered the absurdly fortuitous shot that killed Agent Fields in the armory, and how unruffled he acted in chalking it all up to luck.

"T'zvi?" Charity sounded equally stunned.

"Same team? Afraid not. I'm here for the chip. Open the safe."

"It's not in there," I said.

"Open it!" I complied and moved away when he ordered me to back off to his left. He kept his weapon trained on me and took an eyes-only look inside. He seemed agitated and his eyes seemed almost manic.

"That's one hundred and seventy-five thousand dollars, T'zvi," I said quickly, hoping to distract him. "I know how tough it's been for you all these years and I won't whisper a peep to anyone about this, not even your brother." His eyes stared avidly at the pile. "Take it,' I said. "You've got it coming."

"I'll get lots more than that with the Sabo chip. Hand it over."

"I wish I could. I want to end all this. My work is done here. I want to go home. I never had a beef with you T'zvi, you know that."

I hoped he would lower his guard. But inside I was still reeling from the fact that he had completely turned. It just didn't figure.

"T'zvi, please don't do this," asked Charity. "It's not you. How can you betray Ze'ev… your twin brother? Come on… really?"

"Shut up," T'zvi retorted. "You two have ruined everything, all my plans. I ought to simply kill you both, but I can't. Not yet…"

"Ruined *your* plans?" Charity shook her head in confusion. "All we wanted to do is save this man from killers."

T'zvi walked up to Sabo, pointed the Jericho pistol directly at his head and —*inexplicably*— pulled the trigger.

Blam!

Then he swung it back to cover me, as the banker crumpled. "You just failed to save him. No matter… he meant nothing to us."

"You're crazy," I said, raising my hands and backing away toward the safe. "If you wanted the chip, it made absolutely no sense to harm Sabo." I looked in his eyes. He was high as a kite on something. "Please tell me you did not hurt *Anjela*. Where is she?"

"She ran away, Phillip. I think somehow she knew. I'm sorry you became involved. I like you. These *Ticos* can be vindictive. I told *Aguilera* not to let Sabo's daughter contact you, but he insisted on playing foolish games. You disgraced him the last time you came here."

"You're wrong. I barely made it back alive."

"Perhaps… but you beat his best men and exposed our weapons deals with Voshe to the American government. That cost us millions…"

"Well his revenge game backfired, didn't it? And now that you have killed Sabo, there is no way to find the chip. Was that part of your game plan, too?" I was bluffing of course. I wanted him to believe me, but I was playing a dangerous game. He was acting irrational already and by his actions I knew something insidious was affecting his mind… "T'zvi, the men you're working with are evil. Whatever they got you hooked on, we can help. All this can be cleaned up, and it will be. Ze'ev and I will see to it."

"I don't want your help! I despise him and everything he stands for. We want the chip. We want the money, all of it."

"I can't believe you'd do this to Ze'ev," I said, "after everything…"

"Everything?" His eyes widened. "I *lost* everything. I watched for twenty years as he, the great hero, hopped from place to place and left me to rot in obscurity. I was the chosen one! He was nothing but a brutish killer. The bomb that went off in *Buenos Aires* was meant for him, not me! Did he ever tell you that? He escaped free and clear and everything I ever worked for turned to ashes. Then he left me behind, all these years. I would never have done that to him. Don't you see that my brother and *Vespula* are alike? Trained killers. But she… she changed everything… and now we will have everything together."

"She?"

Chava Cresca appeared in the doorway of the study, armed with her rifle. "That would be me. T'zvi, come over and stand next to me."

T'zvi followed her instructions.

"Keep your gun trained on Phillip. If he moves, shoot him… then shoot the woman."

"You too…?" The hits just kept on coming.

"Sorry, Phillip. You're better than most. Now move and face the wall… hands behind your head, fingers interlaced, and carefully drop to your knees… good… now cross your ankles… well done." She changed her position slightly. "You are free to look at me, now."

"You're good, Chava. You're very good." That's all I could think to say. It seemed inadequate to express my disillusionment.

"I try, like you," she said. Chava then trained her weapon upon Charity. "But unlike you, Phillip, I have no streak of compassion."

"I get that," I said.

"You see, I have a gut feeling that you know the location of the chip, but that you would never tell me. You are a patriot. You would rather die than betray your country and expose it to bio-terror."

"I'm flattered you recognize my sensibilities," I said.

"I'm not counting on your sensibility. I'm counting on your sensitivity… for this beautiful young lady here."

"Leave her alone…"

"No. Look at her, Phillip. She is so appealing and clever, and blessed with a figure to die for. She's a stunning woman, and we both know how you like your women to be stunning…"

"I prefer loyalty… it travels better and lasts longer."

"True. But how many women would follow you half-way around the world, and fight like a mink to keep you safe? And how *sensible* is her loyalty if she is dead? So now we circle back, to examine your sensitivity... to test your feelings for her."

"She's got nothing to do with this," I said.

"Oh, but she does. What will you tell her father and her little son if I plant a bullet in her pretty head right now?"

"Chava..." I did not like the turn of the game.

"...Would you tell them that you had the power to save her, but you chose not to? Would you praise her loyalty at her funeral?"

"You win, Chava. You're calling the shots again. I'll talk."

"All too sensible of you."

"By the way, how did you kill Mrs. Sabo?"

"Batrachotoxin on her cigarette... frog poison, from Columbia... paralysis, then a quick, painless death... I like when people die with their eyes open. But enough! Where is the Sabo chip?"

"Right there in that television. Inside its SD memory card slot."

"Where exactly."

"Only I know where. Your one-handed partner here shot Sabo dead, so he's not telling anyone... not very sensible. He's really not right for you. Perhaps we could share the spoils together... the two of us."

"Together? The two of us?" She laughed contemptuously. "You're good, too. But not *that* good." She gestured with her gun toward Charity. "I'm like her, I detest triangular relationships. T'zvi is the same way. That's why he eliminated her husband, Agent Fields. He got greedy and suggested what you just suggested. T'zvi does not like to share me. He showed fine restraint in the *Pinz*, looking at the back of your head all that time."

"Fine. This is your game. Your rules. So I will simply ask... please let Charity go? You have my word the chip is yours. Would you grant me that small concession?"

"Yes."

"Thank you. There are a few thousand dollars in the safe. T'zvi has seen it there himself. I'd like her to have that too. It will get her home, and it may help with her autistic son. I've caused her nothing but trouble since I came here. May I please give it to her, Chava. That's all I ask and nothing more."

"Fine." I went to reach into the safe, but she stopped me.

"No... first the chip."

"I walked to the television and used my thumbnail to scrape at the small metal logo that covered the SD chip slot. The metal logo came off with relative ease. I popped the chip out, held it up for Chava to see, and laid it down on a nearby coffee table. I looked at the lifeless bodies of the Sabos, one seated and the other draining out into the floor carpet, and then looked at Chava. "...Well?"

"Charity... go to the safe." Charity complied, and when she reached it, Chava said, "Get the money. Drop it into the front of your shirt, and afterwards I will let you go. Do it carefully... T'zvi, pick up the chip, and come over here next to me, but keep your gun pointed at Phillip and never take your eyes off him. If he moves his hands or feet, shoot."

T'zvi walked over, picked up the Sabo chip, and walked backward towards Chava. He handed her the chip and she reached for it with her left hand. At that point I did not know what Charity would do. I simply stared at Chava the whole time.

Chava moved to place the chip in her left breast pocket, and in that instant Charity pulled the compact SIG Sauer 9mm from the *Hercules* safe, pointed the barrel at Chava Cresca and fired twice.

Blam! Blam!

The bullets struck her in the chest. She cried out, "Oh," and her GK36 erupted with gunfire as her right hand spontaneously reacted to her being shot. A violent spray of blood flew out of T'zvi Pinsky's abdomen and he flew forward as if hit from behind by a bus. He landed flat upon his face and did not move. Charity dropped the Sig Sauer to the floor and moaned. I rushed over to Chava as she trembled on her feet and cradled her as she collapsed toward the floor. I laid her down gently. Her eyes looked fearful, and her face paled in the most pitiable way imaginable.

"It was stupid," I said.

I realized that she had purposefully missed *Vespula* that morning. It was no accident. She wanted things to happen as they did. Hers was a warning shot, and she apparently killed *Aguilera*'s female bodyguard on his orders, for whatever reason. I would never know the story of why she turned. It did not matter; she did, but her reasons did not.

Charity walked over and knelt down beside us, and then suddenly burst into tears at the sight of the wounds she had inflicted. She was emotionally traumatized, a bowl of Jell-O, quivering, and more upset than I at the sight of Chava's wounds.

"I'm so sorry!" she cried. "I didn't want to, I swear..."

"...Good shooting," I said, bewildered, and frankly devastated.

"I had to. I saw that gun in the safe... I thought they would kill you, like they did the others. I thought that I... that we... would lose you, and I was so mad at her for betraying you. So I..."

She burst into tears again. She had killed, close up and personal, and *that* can be a whole 'nother ball game, especially the first time.

"You did the right thing, Charity. The chip is more valuable than any of our lives. If she had known its entire contents, I don't think..." Again, all of that didn't matter anymore. The incomparable Chava Cresca lay dying. "It was all so stupid..." I watched as the life ebbed out of her, as the candle flame diminished and the light faded away. She was surely the most beautiful woman I had ever encountered. Then emotionally, as difficult as it was, I let her go.

I retrieved the Sabo chip from her left breast pocket.

"What happens now?"

"We survived. They did not. They stay, we go." I looked directly into Charity's eyes. "It's that simple. No tears for fears. You did the absolute right thing, and I am proud of you. You might want to wipe your fingerprints from the handgun, though."

Charity nodded, sniffled and wiped her nose. "You liked her..."

"Yes." I said. I looked again at Chava's face. "But she made bad choices. For riches, people will do stupid things, and evil things..."

I heard a muffled sound and a groan and looked behind me.

T'zvi had recovered and rolled to his right side. He now faced us. I could see two exit wounds just below his stomach, and they bled profusely. He raised his Jericho pistol and pointed it at my face. I instinctively moved to shield Charity from his wrath and he painfully adjusted his aim to keep me in harm's way.

"She is gone because of you... because you came back. Your turn now, Phillip... your bloody turn now." But before he fired, an old Mayan stone bowl with plumed birds etched into its sides, crashed down and shattered his head. He never moved again.

Anjela stood over his dead body, breathing hard.

Spike stood at her feet... he sidestepped T'zvi's dead body and daintily trotted to me, mildly perturbed. I pet him, and nodded gratefully at *Anjela*. It was the second time she had smashed something over the head of one of my adversaries. I wondered if she realized the coincidence.

"You fight for me," she said. "I fight for you. *Siempre!*"

———

After hearing my story, CIA Agent Walker debriefed me for an hour more aboard the *Freedom*. I learned that the chip's contents were now in the hands of the National Security Agency. The millions in the offshore bank account would aid Costa Rica, currently under siege by the Columbian and Mexican drug cartels. The terrorists listed on the chip would be dealt with in various ways. Some followed, some arrested, some eliminated, until the last remnants of Osama bin Laden's network could be uprooted.

All traces of my presence in Costa Rica, and that of my colleagues would be scrubbed. I could not argue with that.

"The only real question now, is what happened to *Aguilera*," said

Walker. "We found the body of *Vespula*, what remained at least, and identified him through forensic means. He is done. His supply of the deadly virus has been recovered. The Sabo family, including the daughter... all gone. No real loss there, rest assured. *Aguilera's* professional career is over. He is thoroughly exposed. We believe he is on the run or in hiding. We will find him, though, eventually."

"I don't think you will..." I said.

Agent Walker cocked his head. "You know something?"

...I certainly did.

Sometimes the mind plays tricks. You think you've seen somebody, but maybe you haven't. Or have you? I've been there before.

Within half an hour of Chava's death, the three of us had driven four miles to *Playa Herrudura*, another beach town. We left the *Pinz* parked at a pool hall called *Ochos Peletas,* with a signaling chip inside. We purchased an old, Ford Focus right off the street with cash on hand.

As we drove off, *Anjela* declared, "I hungry."

"Me too," I said. I had not eaten in a day. "I'm starving. What about you, Charity?" She nodded, glumly.

"*Pescado*," said *Anjela*.

I liked that. Fish sounded good.

We stopped at a place called *Juanita's*. It was big and spacious and had a nice bar. After we got seated deep in a corner, a tour group arrived too, so the place filled up.

It's my nature to keep looking around in crowded places. Halfway through our meal, as I scanned some tables beyond the bar, my eyes spotted a man's straw fedora hat. It was the only hat in the place and the rain had stopped some time before. My eyes moved on, but then came back as I took a sip of coffee. The head turned, and under the hat's brim I saw a cruel set of dark eyes.

An alarm went off in my head. I slid the car keys to *Anjela*. 'Go get it,' I said with my eyes. She rose without a word.

Charity had since returned the .32 Tomcat I had provided her early on. It was loose in my pocket. I rose and walked down the length of the bar with my hand in that pocket. I was *listo*... ready to go.

I passed the corner of the bar and turned to where I had seen the straw fedora hat and the hard set of eyes. Nothing... the table was empty. He was gone. I glanced in all directions, using the mirror to widen my scope... nothing still. I checked out the men's *baño*... clear. I exited, looked inside the neighboring *baña*, and entered it too... clear.

I knew I was not seeing things.

I returned to *that* table.

I spotted a black matchbook and picked it up... it was half-spent. I turned it over. The matchbook depicted a bright green bird with long tail feathers.

Well, well...

It was from *El Quetzal,* the small Aztec-themed restaurant in *Limon.* I studied the artwork, as I had before, and then rejoined Charity at the table. "Time to fly," I said.

"I boxed up my fish for Spike. I could not eat it."

"Very thoughtful," I said, and then added, "It takes time, but you will feel better." *Anjela* was waiting outside the entrance. I kept my darker thoughts to myself.

An hour later we were on the *Costanera* Highway, or *Ruta* 34, heading for *Capulln* and approaching the *Tárcoles* River. I contacted Temple using his 'calling card'.

"I'm glad you made it out," I said. I filled him in on the fate of Sabo, T'zvi and Chava Cresca.

"Very well," he said, in a most professional and indifferent tone. "We will exit immediately upon your arrival to *Capulln.* You were wise to ditch the *Pinz,* it will be retrieved. I have little doubt you also secured the notebook computer?"

"It's here…"

"Exercise extreme caution, brother man. T'zvi and Chava had access to *the Pinz* and everything in it, including my notebook computer. We must consider it compromised. Pull the car over. Remove the battery and ensure there are no periphery devices attached. Under no circumstances turn it on. Do you understand?"

I did as told. But I was compelled to contact him again.

"The computer was on, even though it was closed. I found a thumb drive, too. Keep it or toss it?"

"Keep it, Phillip. It could prove informative. However, also keep in mind it could have been used to track you, as could the notebook. I am sure you remain cognizant and alert at all times. Have you tried to contact Ze'ev Pinsky?"

"No…"

"Good, don't. He wants to be left alone. I will explain in person. By the way, Phillip, you should enjoy crossing the *Tárcoles* River. It has a large population of the black caiman basking on the shores."

"Caiman?"

"Yes, carnivorous reptiles… crocodiles actually, large and quite impressive… You'll see them for yourself. Or ask *Anjela*, she can tell you all about them, I'm sure— and tell that obstinate young lady that Temple cheerily said, 'Godspeed'."

The crocodiles of Costa Rica did line the river, especially wherever bridges allowed easy human access to the water. They grew big with human feeding, enhanced by constant money-making tours. On the south bank of the river, before we crossed the *Costanera* Highway Bridge, we spied a tour guide feeding a gigantic specimen as a crowd watched. He held a fish high to make the twenty-foot giant rise and snap for its meal. Then the guide fell down in the mud. The crocodile advanced hungrily. It was all dramatics. The guide never looked in danger. Still, I had no desire to get up close to a black caiman, hungry or otherwise. So we continued on, across the bridge, which measured just two lanes wide.

We saw no traffic when we began our brief trek across the *Tárcoles*, but as we approached the bridge's opposite end, a large powerful looking forklift machine rolled into view. It was actually a huge tire manipulator, the type used to change tires on massive construction vehicles.

A huge, square, tong-like clamp held a black rubber tire in its massive grip, a tire wider than a tall man's height. The machine's hydraulic clamping system could roll, lift and turn the tire in every direction imaginable.

"What is that?" asked Charity. What's it doing?"

"It's a tire manipulator, I said. It changes big tires and rims, like the ones on that huge Tonka truck over there...see it?"

"Oh my God, its *big*!"

"Indeed... I got to operate a big truck like that once."

"Really?"

"Yes, when I first got out of the Army and before I went federal. A friend's dad owned a construction company. It was twenty-five feet high and about fifty feet long and it weighed two hundred tons empty..."

"My God," said Charity again, marveling. She had the hint of a smile on her face, and I was glad to see it. I missed that smile. "And this... big tire 'thingy'..."

"Tire manipulator, Charity," I said. "It's not a 'thingy'. It can lift it, spin it, and twist it, anything you want. You'd be surprised."

"And all it does is change the tires on *that* thing over there."

"Well, no... it's like a giant multitasking forklift. Those huge clamps can be changed out for some other tool if you want, but for now it's a just tire manipulator. It's like changing the tool on a vacuum cleaner... same thing, just bigger."

"How much do the tires weigh?"

"Three tons? Depends on the size I guess... I'm just wondering what the contraption is doing way over here?"

The machine robotically swung the gargantuan tire to the side and slammed it down on the road, roughly, temporarily blocking the opposite lane. The cab was rotational; it could turn in a complete circle. The operator had his back to us. The long-armed clamp shifted and moved jerkily, then swung left and right at random. The strong engine revved, and then the arms began their strange jerky movements again.

"Goodness, gracious, what is he doing," asked Charity.

"I don't know… looks like he's in basic training or something." We laughed. "First day on the job, maybe?"

The machine and the long-armed clamps froze.

"Oops," said Charity. "I hope you didn't offend it."

The great machine spun and faced us. Suddenly it lurched forward and stopped. *Anjela* and Charity both screamed, and then the massive, powerful clamps slapped together, crushing both sides of the Ford Focus.

The front windshield crumpled and loosened from its rubberized frame, and the doors and side fenders caved in like plastic jugs. The long-armed clamp easily lifted The Focus off the ground.

I think I yelled, too.

I stepped on the gas pedal, but the wheels just spun in the air. It was like being picked up by King Kong or a Transformer.

I looked into the cab and saw the face of the operator.

Aguilera!

I have no idea how he tracked us, but I knew in that instant that his eyes had met mine at the restaurant in *Playa Herrudura*. He still had on the straw fedora and had the most evil look in his eyes. I waited for him to crush the Focus like a cardboard box… but he didn't.

Charity and *Anjela* screamed again when he began moving the car toward the side of the bridge… toward the river… and the crocodiles.

"He's gonna toss us!" I yelled.

Charity tried to open her door. It was useless. The monster clamp held the front doors tight shut. *Anjela* could open hers in the back. I unbuckled my seatbelt. "Get out, get out, get out!" I shouted. "Hurry, Charity, out through the back!"

Anjela jumped out of the car's back passenger door.

Aguilera had succeeded in lifting the Ford Focus three feet off the ground by then. Charity scrambled to the back seat and tried to exit the same way, but by then that side of the Focus had already been pinned against the highway's safety railing.

"The other door!" I shouted, and she moved to the other side.

At that moment, *Aguilera* hoisted the car a bit higher, so it could clear the railing. When he moved the car slightly more, I felt the tires catch on the top of the safety rail.

On a wing and a prayer, I shifted the transmission down to first gear and floored the gas pedal. Thanks in part to *Aguilera*'s inept skills in operating the clamp, the tires took hold on the railing and began burning rubber.

I punched the gas again and threw the Focus in reverse. The engine screamed bloody murder and the tires burned rubber again. I *almost* broke free, and I can't say what would have happened if I had. But *Aguilera* tightened his grip and lifted the car even higher.

Charity had jumped free. I didn't care what happened to me.

I lifted my body out of my seat, planted my rump in the center console area and kicked out at the windshield with both legs. It blew out and landed on the warped hood of the car.

I dove onto the hood, rose quickly to my feet and leaped onto a section of the clamp. Then I leaped again onto the cab, and faced *Aguilera* directly. He seemed both shocked and outraged by my athleticism. He had opened the clamp when I first landed; the Focus had tipped over the railing and fallen. I heard it splash as I sprang to the machine's clear cab door. I had been in this type of rodeo before, of course.

Only now, it was personal.

I leaped to the side of the cab and grappled at the door.

I swung it open. *Aguilera* punched my face. I took the hit, grabbed his throat, and choked him with all the strength in my right hand. He threw his shoulder at me as I gripped his thick, dark hair, and we both tumbled off the machine. I twisted as we fell to ensure that I landed on top. We hit the ground swinging but the advantage belonged to me.

I pounded his face bloody until he abandoned combat and merely defended himself from the blows.

Then I relented, and stood up. I looked down at him in disgust. I wanted to take him alive.

"Get up *Aguilera* you bastard!"

He did, slowly, and smiled. His back was to the railing; my back was to the machine...

"You want more of me, don't you," he said, wiping blood from his mouth. "You want more because I beat you down, eh Gringo! Yankee filth! This is my country, not yours! I'll have everyone in your family cut to pieces... do you hear me! Do you?"

He was staggering with rage.

"You liked the Israeli whore... I had her first. I owned her completely. You like the Sabo whores too... the young one told me how you looked at her with your little beady eyes... I preferred her mother." He laughed derisively. "You will not leave this country alive... *never!*"

"I listened to the radio on the way here, *Aguilera*. You should too. You are through. You are wanted by your own government. If you go back... they'll arrest you, or the cartels will kill you. You hurt me, but I've hurt you far more. I saw you fall from your high perch, and here I am, still standing."

He reached for his shoulder holster. "I'll kill you!"

I saw the move coming before he even thought to try.

His hand never touched the gun. I spun and kicked, my foot landing on the corner of his left jaw bone. He flew backwards, hit the rail and fell over it. He screamed, and landed in the water. He survived the fall. But he did not survive the host of black caiman that responded to his thrashings. He saw them coming, and looked about, then made a splash at trying to swim.

It was hopeless and he knew it.

An alpha male struck first, from beneath him, grabbing his leg as he screamed. It began to roll and spin, over and over, as *Aguilera* screeched and bellowed, and then fell silent. He floated. One leg had been severed. Other big caiman began drifting in for their share.

I felt no pity... none at all.

I took a deep breath. "See ya later, Alligator."

I was standing on the deck of the *Freedom* with Walker, the CIA man, when Ze'ev Pinsky's helicopter came into view.

"Are you mad at him for not telling you about the full contents of the chip?"

"No," I said. "I was, but not anymore. It would have changed my interactions with people, and maybe the way I operated. I mean, essentially, it's all in the game, right? Plus... he lost a brother."

"Maybe he found one, too."

I nodded. "Thank you for the fresh perspective."

"By the way, Mr. Sheppard... although your actions were not sanctioned and will be disavowed, I and others like me have been impressed by your perseverance, your bravery, and your effectiveness. The elimination of *Vespula*, the exposure of terrorist networks, and the call to final reckoning of corrupt officials and agents is no insignificant achievement. I am proud to know you. Would you be amenable to working with us in the future on certain projects, on the same basis of secrecy, anonymity and deniability? There are times and places where your unique abilities would be useful."

"Why not? I am a Specialist."

"Indeed." Agent Walker pulled out a cigarette. He tried to light it with a *Bic*, but it would not go. I turned my back to the wind, produced a black matchbox, and provided him a light of his cigarette. His eyes scanned the artwork on the matchbox as I shielded the flame from the wind. "Hmm... that's a *Quetzal* bird, is it not?" I nodded. He drew in deeply, and then exhaled into the sea breeze. "Beautiful birds... that's nice artwork too."

I nodded again. "I like it... I like it a lot."

CPSIA information can be obtained at www.ICGtesting.com
Printed in the USA
LVOW062138240413

330853LV00001B/39/P